OOPS, I ELF'D IT AGAIN

MONSTERVILLE, USA, BOOK 7

AVA ROSS

OOPS, I ELF'D IT AGAIN

Monsterville, USA 7

Copyright © 2023 Ava Ross

Cover art by Wolfraven Studio

Editing/Proofreading by JA Wren & Owl Eyes Proofs & Edits

*For my parents & family who
always believed I could do this.*

SERIES BY AVA

Mail-Order Brides of Crakair

Brides of Driegon

Fated Mates of the Ferlaern Warriors

Fated Mates of the Xilan Warriors

Holiday with a Cu'zod Warrior

Galaxy Games

Alien Warrior Abandoned

Beastly Alien Boss

Bride of the Fae

A Sci-Fi Holiday Tail

Monsterville, USA

Monster on Board
(co-written with Alana Khan)

A Monster Worth Fighting For
(Monster Between the Sheets)

Love at First Orc

Third Galaxy on the Left

Monster Mate Hunt

You can find her books on Amazon.

OOPS, I ELF'D IT AGAIN

I'm teaching a gorgeous elf how to fit in with humans and now I'm falling in love.

With thirty-six looming on my horizon, I'm determined to have a child. I don't need romance. I don't need love. And I definitely don't need a happily ever after.

When my friend talks me into attending an elf ball at an estate in Monsterville, promising I'll find a guy there who'll give me what I'm seeking, I agree to go with her.

I'm barely there when I fall into the arms of the most gorgeous elf I've ever seen, Tylik. He's the LOTR elf of my dreams, so it's a good thing I've sworn off romance.

Tylik needs someone to teach him how to fit in with human society. I need a bundle of joy. We'll help each other, then end things with no looking back.

But between teaching Tylik how to drive and showing him that ice cream is amazing, I fall in love. What if he doesn't feel the same?

Oops, I Elf'd it Again, Book 7 in the Monsterville, USA Series, is a spicy monster romcom. Each book is stand-alone and best if read in order (see below). Expect romantic hijinks with monsters, heat, and a happily ever after.

Check out the entire Monsterville world!

Candy for my Orc Boss
Orc Me Baby One More Time
Gargoyles Just Want to Have Fun
Don't Go Knotting My Heart
Whose Bed Have Your Claws Been Under?
Uptown Ogre
Oops, I Elf'd it Again
My Orc-y Breaky Heart
Hold Me Closer, Fiery Phoenix
Who Let the Demon Out?

CHAPTER 1
KATE

I was not a princess, but I was going to a ball. An elf ball! My bestie, Seyla, hoped to find someone to love. As for me, I was looking for a baby daddy.

We rode in the back of a Lyft, the driver taking the main road into the mountains surrounding Monsterville, aiming for the elf duchess's estate. Our puffy gowns billowed around us, and my feet ache from the tiny slippers Seyla had insisted I wear to this illustrious event.

They'd built the estate in the hills with the help of an orc guy who owned a construction company in town, adding a dash of magic. How else could it have been erected so quickly?

Anticipation rocketed through my belly, and Seyla must've felt the same because she kept wrangling my hand and grinning.

Our troll driver peered at us in his rearview mirror. Pressing down on the gas pedal, he urged the vehicle up a winding road, slowly taking us through the dense forest where I'd heard wolf shifter packs and a yeti still lived.

We'd cracked a window, and warm, summery air billowed across us, cooling my overheated body. The fresh scent of pine trees filled my senses, and when we reached the peak of one of the lower hills, we spied our destination; the gilded, four-story building perched on the top of one of the crests.

"Tell me again why we're doing this?" I said for what had to be the thousandth time.

When Seyla smiled, the dimple in her right cheek showed. "Because we're Cinderella without the stepsisters. Commoners attending an elf ball."

"We're human, not necessarily commoners."

She sniffed. "To the elves, we're probably very common."

"The elves are probably right." Regarding me anyway. My upbringing had been simple and poor, though that wasn't uncommon in this country.

As for Seyla, she was wealthy, though you wouldn't know it. My friend was anything but snooty.

"Tonight, you're a princess," she said. "I'll be your lady's maid."

"Ha ha. More like the other way around."

She rolled her pretty brown eyes framed with incredibly long lashes and smoothed her long brown hair shot through with naturally golden highlights. If she wasn't such a nice person, I'd hate her for her lashes alone. To make mine look good, I had to wear fifty coats of mascara or attach fake ones. And forget brown hair gleaming in the sunlight. I was stuck with the same auburn as my mom.

"I'm worried I'm going to trip and fall in this gown," I said. "You know I don't do fancy." I was more a jeans and t-shirt kind of girl.

"I'll hold on to you."

Until she was surrounded by guys, the norm with my friend. She would barely see them, and she'd be embarrassed to draw their attention. Meanwhile, I'd awkwardly lurk in the shadows of her light despite her trying to drag me into the sunshine to stand beside her. "It's nice to look pretty every now and then, isn't it?"

"It is."

She leaned against my shoulder. "Thank you for coming with me."

Our vehicle swooped down the hill and up the next, and in no time, we glided along a long, paved drive leading to the enormous, ancient-appearing structure. I pressed my face against the window, taking in the huge blocks of white stone making up the soaring stone walls with spires on each corner. A lush green meadow surrounded the castle with a dense forest behind. Rays from the setting sun slanted across the sky, highlighting colorful flowerbeds scattered throughout the landscape.

"We're going to a ball, and I'm going to find the monster of my dreams," she said. "No ifs, ands, or buts."

Ah, monsters . . .

A few years ago, they'd crawled out of the woods and announced they'd been living parallel lives to ours. At first, everyone freaked. I mean, who wouldn't when an orc stomped through town? This explained the yeti sightings through the years, let alone the Loch Ness Monster. They were *all* real. A treaty was formed, and they moved in among us, the majority of them settling in this area.

When Seyla had suggested we move to Monsterville, I'd snickered. But when she'd talked about meeting a nice monster to love forever, I'd caved. I didn't want a long-term relationship, but I'd never hold her back.

It didn't really matter where I lived as long as I was near my best friend.

"You know I'm not looking for a boyfriend or husband," I said. When you loved someone, they left you, like my dad. "I've got one goal." At thirty-five, my clock was ticking. "My eggs are aging and it's time to put one of them to good use."

"Lots of women have kids when they're older, even in their fifties. And if you can't carry one yourself, you can hire a surrogate or try adoption. There are tons of foster kids looking for someone to love."

"I'm not opposed to any of that, but I've set a goal. I can accomplish anything I want to as long as I put my mind to it."

"Your determination is amazing."

"Thank you."

"We'll find a baby daddy for you at the ball." She squinted out the window as the vehicle approached the castle. "If there are no likely prospects, we'll cut out early and watch some movies."

"Mermaid first, I assume."

"Then we'll watch Brave."

My favorite.

"I see myself as Princess Merida—minus the cute shape and princess-ness," I said.

"You're regal."

"Thanks." I stroked my long tresses she'd artfully arranged for me. She said pulling them up made my neck appear swanlike. "I've got her hair."

"Totally."

"It's my one good feature."

"You have tons of good features." She pursed her lips. "You're pretty, brave like the princess, and you're the nicest person I know." She poked my chest gently.

"We just moved to Monsterville so we don't know many people here." We'd packed our things and driven halfway across the country, renting rooms at a cute little B&B run by a human/gargoyle couple, Violet and Goreg. I missed my mom, but it was time I stretched my wings.

Seyla had put a deposit on a house and would move out soon. I'd remain at the B&B until I'd saved enough for an apartment. The B&B wasn't a bad place to live. Eye candy helped; Goreg was a god with wings.

"You know what I mean," she said. "You're amazing. Some monster is going to scoop you up."

"I think the phrase is sweep me off my feet."

"That too."

I shot her a grin. "Thanks, but nope."

"You need to saddle that bad boy and get riding."

"Men are not stallions."

"Around here, they might be. Have you checked out the centaur living down the street?"

I frowned. "I've always wondered about centaurs."

"Ask one on a date. It could be a wild ride."

We both snickered. Talking about a guy's junk was much easier than dealing with it.

"You look wonderful, and every elf in the place is going to notice," she said. "Our gowns are perfect. *We're* perfect."

Thank you, Rylee, for giving me a full-time position —with benefits! —in her cupcake shop/bakery. Otherwise, I wouldn't have been able to afford this gown, even with Seyla's "loan" that wasn't really a loan. As a romance author, she made boatloads of money. She'd paid for half my dress.

I'd have more money in general but my mom needed help. There was nothing wrong with being there for your family.

"I think this is as close as I'm allowed to go," the troll driver said, bringing the vehicle to a stop behind other vehicles discharging guests. "Is this enough?"

"Yes, thanks," I said.

"The elf ball, then, my ladies," he said, sweeping his clawed hand toward the huge stone estate.

"Thank you," Seyla called out in a sing-song voice. "Here we come, elves!"

I liked elves. Lord of the Rings was one of my favorite movies.

The driver backed up and turned, soon zooming down the drive while Seyla and I tiptoed toward the entrance on our heels. We took the broad granite steps to the top and followed other guests toward the big front doors held open by elves with long black hair and pristine tunics with enough gild to fit in a medieval movie.

Seyla paused on the broad stone deck to primp our hair and dresses.

Two elf women to our right glared.

"You're in the way," one said, staring down her hawk-like nose at us.

I gaped at her long, glorious white hair, her teal eyes that almost glowed, and how amazing she looked in her silver gown.

"Come, Drueline," the other woman said in a snooty tone, tugging on her friend's arm. "Ignore the humans."

They sauntered through the front door like runway models.

"Yeah, we'll ignore *them*," Seyla said, fluffing the artfully created curls draping around my shoulders. "Funny how you run into mean girls in every culture. You'd think women would stand up for each other, but no." She smoothed my gown and grinned. "It doesn't matter. You're pure perfection."

"Thanks. So are you."

"You'll find someone tonight. Curl your finger a likely guy's way, take him to the garden for some hot and heavy, then say goodbye."

"I can't do something like that. That would be using someone as a sperm donor without his consent."

"Be honest, then. Tell him you want a baby, but you

don't want commitment, that you won't ask him for child support or any rights."

I frowned. "Will a guy go along with something like that?'

She shrugged. "All you can do is ask."

Short of putting up a notice on the telephone poles in town, *Woman Seeking Sperm Donor, only those uninterested in commitment need apply*, I didn't appear to have many options.

I doubted Monster Mingle, the matchmaking business in town, would fix me up with a monster looking to give me a baby without the marriage, house, and backyard stuff that made my heart eager to run.

"Consider it a bachelorette season only instead of looking for a husband, you're looking for baby-making material."

"No love."

She made an X on her chest. "Emotions are off limits. Make that clear from the start."

As we passed the elves holding the doors open, they bowed. We tap-tap-tapped on our heels into an enormous, multi-story foyer. Gold outlined the walls and the arched ceiling three or four stories above us. Magic hung in the air; I could almost feel it shimmering around me.

"That can't be real gold," I whispered to Seyla, nudging my finger toward a satyr statue gleaming in the low lights.

She shrugged and smoothed her gown. She'd dressed in a floor-length, baby blue dress that made her look like a princess.

I wore a dark green dress that was essentially a cliché for a redhead, one with a too-low bodice that barely covered my boobs. As long as I didn't sneeze, they wouldn't pop out.

"Where should we go?" I asked, peering around.

"Up the stairs, ladies," one of the tall elves near the door said, pointing. "Follow the sounds of the crowd." His appreciative gaze glided down Seyla's body, though she didn't appear to notice.

At the top of the stairs, we walked sedately down an ornate hall with marble tiled floors and paintings of stoic elves mounted on the walls. At the end, we came to a large double doorway with huge planters on either side containing potted palms reaching toward the high ceiling. Lilting music, bright chatter, and the clink of glasses drew us toward the room beyond like butterflies to pretty flowers.

We paused in the opening, eyeing the ball in progress.

"Whoa. Monsters," Seyla breathed, taking in golden-furred yetis, short trolls with knobby heads, ogres, orcs, and so many other kinds of monsters I quickly lost count.

And so many elves. Universally tall, they had long hair of every color imaginable, and the males wore tunics that would fit into a fantasy movie. The women wore gowns like ours. They were regal, they stole my breath.

One elf guy caught my eye. He towered over the rest, his broad shoulders filling out his deep blue tunic that matched his sapphire eyes. Some of his silver hair had been pulled up in a man bun at the back of his head, leaving the rest draping around his shoulders. Thranduil anyone?

As if he sensed my attention, his gaze scanned the room and locked on mine. He continued to stare. Heat filled my cheeks. Women of various species fluttered around him, and I could see why. I kinda wanted to hover around him myself.

He disengaged himself from the women and left the ballroom through a door on side before I could head in his direction.

"It's gorgeous here," Seyla sighed.

A table holding drinks and snacks had been set up along the left wall, and I'd head in that direction as soon as one of the numerous monsters staring Seyla's way snagged her attention. A majestic fountain containing a beverage took up the center of the table, guests dipping out glasses before rejoining the crowd.

The far wall was made up of multi-story glass, it overlooked the gardens spreading across an enormous back lawn all the way to the forest. Setting sunlight sparkled on fountains and highlighted numerous statues.

Seyla shot me a nervous smile. "Let's get a drink. I need the boost."

I followed her toward the fountain, but before we got there, a tall, gorgeous elf wearing a dark purple tunic and black pants, with black hair shot through with gold, strutted over to walk beside her.

When she stopped, he bowed and held out his hand. "Would you care to dance?"

She fluttered her hands at her throat and looked at me.

I knew what she was thinking. She didn't want to abandon me.

"Go," I said with an easy smile. "I'll get that drink and hang out."

"You're sure?" she said.

"Totally."

After shooting me a sly grin, she took the elf's hand, and he led her toward the big dance floor in front of the windows.

I skipped the buffet table and drink fountain, scooting along the outside of the room until I reached the door the gorgeous elf had disappeared through.

Because I was curious about where he'd gone, I ducked through the opening, finding myself in a long, gilded hall. I walked along the smooth, marble surface all the way to the end and through a big archway, finding yet another hall stretching to my left and right. After taking a few rights, and then a couple of lefts, I was lost, and no one was ever going to find me.

So much for scouting out potential baby making material.

I was passing yet another open doorway when I spied a giant library through the opening. Totally cool.

Stepping inside, I gasped. I was Belle, and I'd walked into book heaven. Shelves full of colorful books took up three of the four walls of the enormous, multi-story room. On the outer wall, tall windows surrounded with thick ruby drapes looked out at the gardens, and a huge stone fireplace dominated the center of the wall.

I strolled across the right side of the room, tracing my fingers across the spines. So many choices. How could someone decide which to read first?

Voices echoed in the hallway.

Afraid of being caught where I didn't belong, I scurried across the room and ducked behind one of the long, thick drapes.

Someone entered the room, and from the sound, they sat in a chair near the fireplace. Another person joined the first, and his deep, achingly beautiful voice echoed in the room.

I wanted to reveal myself and meet him. He must be one of the painfully gorgeous elves I'd seen in the ballroom.

I waited, remaining still.

Listening.

CHAPTER 2
TYLIK

My great-aunt Finnadestria, or Finni, as she liked to be called, sent word through the estate's staff asking me to join her in the library for a "quick conversation". If I knew my aunt, she would present her thoughts, and I'd do my best to talk her out of them.

"It's time for you to assume your rightful place as duke of my estates in the fae realm," she said the moment I walked into the library. Dressed in an ornate silver silk gown, she sat in one of the brocade chairs flanking the enormous stone fireplace. She waved for me to settle in the other. "You're nearly thirty. You should've taken the title years ago."

"I told you I don't wish to return to the fae realm at this time." Or ever if I could avoid it. I paced across the thick carpet. "I'm happy here."

"How can you be?" She sniffed. "While I can see why someone would be fascinated by this new world, I cannot imagine why you'd want to remain here even as long as you have. You've been here for a month already."

"I've opened an apothecary. My new home has been finished. My life is here."

I should leave. Go to the ball or not. It hardly mattered. But she'd raised me and my sister. She was old, and her health was not good. I loved her. So I sat in the chair beside her, determined to explain in a way she'd understand. "Humans are amazing."

She smiled with a hint of indulgence. "I can see their charm."

"They work and play, and they are so much more alive than elves."

"It's a satisfying trade. We live much longer than them."

"But we only half live." I'd noted this from the moment I arrived. For the first time, I felt everything. The tastes, smells, and sounds lured me in. Now that my eyes had been opened, I didn't want to go back to the deadened existence I'd lived in the fae realm.

"If we experienced everything as fully as a human, we'd burst into flames," she said. "Soon, only cinders would remain."

"No one has proven this rumor. Besides, I'd rather live a shorter life and feel than drone on for many ages only skimming the surface of what life has to offer." Could I make her understand?

"It's frightening, don't you think?" She frowned. "I don't like being awash with my senses all the time. I plan to return to the fae realm soon and the peace I'll find there. You need to come with me."

"I told you. I'm not ready to leave."

"You've been busy. I've heard rumors in town," she said, watching me intently.

"What in particular?"

"I've become friends with a human named Elvira."

Elvira . . . "Grannie Vi?" She was also amazing. This was a new word I'd learned, and I used it often.

"We've had tea twice, and she's a wealth of information about this new community they've named Monsterville."

I was surprised my aunt had stepped beyond the building's front doors.

"I will say, this estate is worthy," she said, though without a hint of superiority. Like most elves, she preferred a world full of magic instead of being here where our spells were so weak they barely made a ripple.

"I'm not surprised. Maxon Zahgorim built it," I said, proud of my friend's efforts.

"Your orc friend has done an excellent job." She dipped her head forward, giving me a slight smile. "See? Monsters, as they call us, and may I say that's an uncouth term for glorious elves, contribute to a *magical* society. Humans are not capable of enjoying magic the way we do. However, the rules are clear. We're not permitted to use our power here except in small ways that have little or no impact."

"What has Grannie Vi been saying?" I asked carefully.

"You visited her new business, Monster Mingle. You wish to join in wedded bliss with a human."

"I do."

I'd gone to Grannie Vi's matchmaking service out of desperation. If I could find a human to marry me, my aunt might "permit" me to remain here forever. As a duchess and a well-respected elf in the fae realm, she could insist, and then I'd have to return home. I was here by her good grace, plus that of the fae council and our ambassador.

However, my great aunt had a soft heart. She wanted me to be happy. If I fell in love, I doubted she'd stand in my way.

I wasn't sure what I'd do with a wife, but it was my only solution. Humans were rarely allowed to enter the fae realm, but if I was mated with one, I'd be allowed to stay here. The guidelines of our treaty made this clear.

Finni's pale eyebrows lifted, and her pointed ears twitched. She fingered the inch-long red stone she wore around her neck on a thick gold chain that matched the rubies peppering her artfully arranged hair. "Why a human?"

"They're fascinating."

"You'll grow bored."

"I don't believe I will."

"I suppose if you had a wife, I might reconsider," she said, a sly look entering her eyes. I wasn't sure how to interpret it, but I welcomed her comment. "I'll give you a week of human time to find her."

My spine stiffened. "Excuse me?"

"Find a human and marry her within one week, and I'll consider allowing you to remain here."

My heart jolted. "A week isn't very long."

"You've been here a month already. Elvira has given you potential matches."

None of them had worked out.

"I'm getting old," Finni said. "I wish to retire. I plan to do so once you assume the dukedom and take my place among our people."

"Allow my sister to become duchess instead."

"Tradition dictates this role should be filled by the eldest, which is you."

"Tradition sucks."

"Language." She tapped my knee, but her eyes sparkled.

"Isirell loves our people, our world," I said. "And *you've* ruled as duchess."

"Because there was no one else in my line."

I was making no progress in convincing her. Frustration poured through me. Rising, I started pacing again. "I'm a grown male. I will do whatever the hell I please."

"Again, language. Please do not invoke demons."

I dipped forward in a bow. "I do apologize. You must know that demons have joined this community. The town's sheriff, Venom, is one of them."

"I'm well aware of Sheriff Venom. He's not exactly from hell, per se, but the underworld."

It was the same thing to me. "Alright," I growled. "I'll find a wife within one week."

"Lovely." Her lips curled up briefly before smoothing.

She must not think I could do it. "I do have one other condition."

Of course she did. I loved her, but damn, did she adore manipulating others. After my parents died, she'd raised me and my sister. She'd been our everything when we'd lost so much.

I'd laughed at times when she twisted someone into agreeing with her wishes. It wasn't funny when her slyness was directed at me.

"What do you wish?" Pausing on the carpet, I braced myself for her words.

"You say you enjoy living in the human realm? Then show me you fit in here."

Ah, so she'd seen how awkward I felt among humans. I used the wrong words and a solid understanding of their cultural aspects eluded me. Too often, they stared or even yelled when I made mistakes. If only I could fit in.

"Find a wife and show me that this is where you truly belong, and I'll release you," my aunt said. "Your sister can take the title of duchess."

Where was I going to find someone to marry me within a week, let alone someone to teach me how to fit in?

"It would take me a human lifetime to learn how to act as they do," I said.

"I will accept attempts in that direction." She rose from her chair. "Perhaps a human bride can help you."

"I will do my best to find her," I said, bowing. At least she was giving me a chance.

"You're a good boy." She paused to tap my cheek. "Now I must attend the ball and see if I can discover why you are so fascinated by these beings." With a wrinkly smile, she left the room.

Groaning, I dropped into the chair she'd vacated and cupped my face in my hands. "How am I going to find someone to marry me so quickly?" Teaching me to fit in seemed like the simplest of the two tasks.

A rustle rang out from the draperies, and a pretty human woman dressed in a green floor-length gown with auburn hair and the most beautiful blue eyes I've ever seen, stepped toward me.

Stopping in front of me, her pale cheeks flushed. "Marry me."

"Excuse me, my lady?"

"I'll marry you and show you how to fit in with human society." More color rose into her face. "I have one condition for our marriage, however. I don't want a long-term relationship. I only want a baby. You can be the daddy."

CHAPTER 3

KATE

"I believe I've misunderstood you, lovely human," he said in a formal tone, sitting up straighter in the brocade chair.

Lovely. So sweet.

Not buying it.

However, this was the elf I'd crushed on in the ballroom. Talk about aiming high.

"I guess I should say I'm sorry before I explain." I cringed because it was never nice to listen in on conversations. "I didn't mean to overhear. I . . . stepped away from the ball for a breath of fresh air." Damn, I was good at this pretty, formal talk. "And I sauntered into the library."

"Sauntered?" He hitched one silver eyebrow, something he shouldn't do because it only made him more devastatingly handsome.

But I could tell by the sparkle in his sapphire eyes that he was teasing me.

For a second, I almost yanked back my offer. What would it be like to be married to this guy, to have his baby, but never claim his heart? From what I'd overheard, he'd be easy to love.

He might be my best option, however.

"Allow me to explain." I sat in the chair beside him.

"Please do." Leaning back, he studied me with a tight brow.

"I overheard, and there's no taking it back. You need a human bride and to learn how to—"

"I don't exactly need a bride."

"The elderly elf lady thinks you do."

"She's my great-aunt," he said. "As you heard, she wants me to return to the fae realm permanently. I wish to remain here. If marrying someone will make this possible, I will marry."

"And I want a baby. I don't need to get married to have one, but if I'm asking you to give me a baby, it's only fair I offer you something in exchange."

"Why do you want a child?"

"Because I love them. I'm thirty-five. My clock is ticking. I don't want love or flowers or wooing. I'm looking for a practical arrangement."

"I do admire frankness," he said thoughtfully.

I grinned. Funny how I could speak with him easily while I fumbled my words with other guys. Perhaps I should've tried to arrange a short-term marriage with them instead.

"I have no expectations from the father," I added. "You wouldn't need to see the child unless you wanted to, and you wouldn't need to give me financial support."

"What if the father wants to be a part of your child's life?"

I tilted my head. "Would *you*?"

He shrugged. "How should I know? I don't have a child."

"Or a fiancée to marry you within one week."

He sighed. "This is a valid point."

"You're gorgeous; there's no denying that. But because I'm not interested in anything permanent, I'll ignore your pretty face and muscular form, plus your long golden hair." Some of which was pulled up in a man bun at the back of his head, the rest draping around his shoulders. "Under any other circumstances, I'd be swooning if you glanced my way."

He huffed. "What *exactly* are you proposing?"

I LEANED TOWARD HIM. "I'll help you fulfill your aunt's request. I'll marry you and teach you how to fit in with humans as long as you agree to give me a child."

"I—"

I held out my hand. "Deal or no deal, Duke?"

He stared down his nose at my hand. "I am not a duke, and if I have any say in it, I never will be."

"You're close to being a duke."

He groaned. "You're right."

I lifted my voice. "Deal or no deal?"

He continued to stare at my hand. "What is this gesture you make?"

"If we clasp hands, it means neither of us can back out without a good reason."

His head tilted, and he studied my face. "You'd have sex with a stranger to have a child?"

I squirmed. Way to make it sound sleazy. "We could do artificial insemination."

His brow drew together. "What's that?"

"Depositing your seed in a cup. It would be inserted inside me by a medical professional."

"I wouldn't want to make a child in that way." A slight smile rose on his face. "Here is *my* proposal, lovely human. You will marry me, and I will give you a child. However . . ."

As if music rose to a crescendo, I knew my life was about to change in ways I'd never imagined.

"However what?" I asked, my voice shaking as hard as my hands.

"We make your baby in the natural way."

TYLIK

What a peculiar, yet intriguing young woman. I studied her gorgeous auburn hair swept up on the back of her head with curled tendrils draping around her shoulders, her lush form I was surprisingly eager to touch, and the nervousness in her eyes.

"Alright, we'll have sex." Frowning, she bit down on her ripe pink lips I wanted to test with my own.

Perhaps I should tell her I was sorry, that I could not fulfill this agreement. If I was attracted to her at our first meeting, how would I follow through with her condition to end the marriage when she was carrying my child?

My cock jerked upward at the thought of giving her a baby, and I could picture her holding it; her face flushed from the delivery, her warm gaze meeting mine. Our child would be beautiful, a mix of her and me, and—

Hold it right there. What the hell was I thinking? I shook my head and focused on the task at hand.

"Any other conditions?" she asked.

"You must move into my home with me. That'll make it simpler for you to teach me how to fit in with humans."

"You'll never completely fit in, and you shouldn't. You're an elf, and you're you. That's special already. But I can help you feel comfortable around humans if that's enough."

"Very well."

"I assume we'll sleep together from the start?"

"I'm willing to delay this until you're comfortable. After all, I have a week before I must marry."

Sleep would be the last thing on my mind if this woman lay beside me.

I wanted to growl. She was offering a contract, not a romantic relationship. Her offer fit perfectly with what I needed. My aunt would stop trying to collar me with the dukedom. She would stop asking me to return to the fae realm.

"You'd have to pretend to feel vague affection for me," I said. "Only to convince my aunt. She'll be suspicious if you don't."

"If we get married within a week, she's going to be suspicious anyway."

"She knows I'll have to find someone quickly. But we can tell her we've known each other since I arrived in your realm. I've been here a month already."

"That might work."

"We can announce our engagement tonight."

"I can handle a quick engagement. And while it sounds cold to tell someone I want a child but that he doesn't need to be a part of the baby's life, it would be your child too. You could see it and be with it as much as you'd like." She swallowed hard. "As I said, I wouldn't expect financial support or anything like that. This is an agreement. I'll marry you and teach you, and you'll give me a baby." Her soft gaze met mine. "I've always wanted to have children. I know many women have them well into their forties, but my arms ache to hold one now. Is that bad?"

"Not at all. I want to be a part of my child's life and provide financial support." I held up my hand. "I won't accept anything else."

She grumbled but nodded.

What would we have, a boy or a girl?

And what was I thinking? How could I plant my seed in this woman's body, then walk away from her?

I'd have to. That was her condition, and I must honor it.

I held out my hand to solidify our contractual obligation.

She placed hers tentatively in mine, and I tried to ignore the heat flaring up my arm from her simple touch.

"Deal?" she asked.

I jerked out a nod and told my damn cock to behave. "We have an agreement, my lady."

CHAPTER 5
KATE

We left the library and walked to the ballroom. Tylik's frown consumed his forehead. Was he having second thoughts already?

"Do you want to back out?" I had to give him the chance.

"Not at all." He took my hand and drew me closer to the ballroom. Music rang out along with chatter. "Do you?"

"No." Perhaps I should. I was attracted to him. We'd sleep together and hang out together until I got pregnant. Could I walk away with my heart intact?

I hadn't expected my baby daddy to want to make the child in the usual way, but it wouldn't be a hardship to sleep with Tylik. The thought sent delicious shivers down my spine.

"My aunt means everything to me," he said. "She raised me, and she only wants to see me happy."

"She sounds like an admirable woman." I hadn't heard enough to make judgment.

"It's important to me that she believes we like each other."

"Alright." It wouldn't have to fake it; I liked him already.

He stopped outside the door to the ballroom. "You'll move in with me soon?"

"How about Thursday? I need to pack and settle a few things." And build a wall around my heart.

"We will . . . sleep together, as you say, from then on?"

"Sure." For a hasty agreement, my body was awfully excited about being intimate with him. "What if it's not the right time for me to get pregnant?"

"Practice?" he said with a devilish grin.

Overheated already, I waved my hand in front of my face.

He took it and kissed my knuckles. "Never believe I don't welcome this task."

This guy was dangerous.

But he was an elf. They came with a rep for enjoying seduction.

More shivers jolted through me from his simple touch. Maybe this was a huge mistake. It was easy to say I didn't want love or romance, but my heart might head down that path and drag me along with it.

"Very well, then." He held out his arm, and when I linked us together, he opened the door and swept me inside. Not stopping, he took me through the center of the room, not skirting around the edges like I would've if I was alone. Don't draw attention, that was my motto.

People parted like we were royalty. Actually, he essentially was.

He took me up onto a platform near the dance floor, where an ogre quartet played odd string instruments. When Tylik lifted his hand, the music came to a halt.

"I have an announcement to make," he said in a booming voice.

It was so quiet you could hear a feather hit the floor.

He held out his hand to his aunt, and she tittered before walking over to join us on the platform.

"Tylik?" she asked, studying me. Thankfully, I didn't see unkindness in her expression. She might judge me, but I sensed she'd be fair in how she did it.

He lifted his voice. "This lovely woman has consented to be my wife."

The elf woman with white hair who'd sneered at us on the front steps stood not far away.

She punctuated his words with a gasp.

"No," she cried, glaring from me to Tylik.

She flicked her arms up in the air, then stormed from the ballroom.

Finni stared after the woman. "Drueline is upset, but such is life." Turning to me, she took my hands, squeezing them. She was so much taller than me, as were all the elves. "A wedding. Such wonderful news."

"Indeed," Tylik said, nodding to me. "In one week's time, I will wed . . ."

My sedate smile faltered.

"I will wed . . ." he said again, his panicked gaze meeting mine.

Oh, shit.

I hadn't told him my name.

CHAPTER 6
TYLIK

"I will wed . . ." What kind of male agrees to marry a woman without even asking her name?

Titters rang out in the room.

I turned a panicked gaze my fiancée's way.

"I'm Katherine Austin Holsom," my future wife announced smoothly to the room.

My surging pulse backed off to a more normal rhythm.

She eased around my aunt and joined me, giving me a caring smile. She was so lovely and understanding about this that she stole the wind from my lungs. Her voice lowered to a whisper. "Call me Kate, though, okay?"

I linked our hands and lifted them, grinning. "This is Kate."

"Kate is a good name," my aunt said, beaming at us both. "It's regal."

I was glad she approved thus far.

"Kate?" I said. "Allow me to introduce you to my aunt, Finnadestria Soliana Niolese Revalor."

"Please call me Finni," my aunt said, taking Kate's hand and patting it. "I'm delighted you've found my beloved nephew."

"Yes." Kate's gaze sought mine. "He's . . . wonderful."

"I'll reach out to Raze and Elisa to handle the event?" My aunt asked.

"Yes, please do." My ogre friend and his human fiancée ran a wedding planning service. No one but them would do.

"When do you plan to wed?" my aunt asked.

Within a week, obviously, though I didn't point that out. "Kate?"

"Next Saturday?"

"That will be perfect," I said. "If you don't mind, Aunt, I'd like to dance with my fiancée to celebrate our engagement."

"Where's her ring?" my aunt asked, studying Kate's bare fingers.

"I thought we could go through the family jewels and select something together." I was getting good at making things up.

"What a delightful idea," my aunt said, tapping her fingertips together. "I'll put them on display, and you can choose. Will Friday be alright? It will take time to bring them all from the fae realm."

I dipped my head forward in agreement.

Kate stared at both of us, but I couldn't read her expression.

"Would you care to dance?" I asked, holding out my hand.

"I thought you'd never ask."

She'd impressed me already with her quick thinking. Perhaps this would go smoother than I could hope.

Under my aunt's watchful gaze, I led my future bride onto the dance floor. Everyone left the smooth surface, elves bowing before stepping backward, humans fluttering and whispering but following their lead.

Kate shot me a nervous smile. She leaned forward, whispering. "I don't know how to do formal dances."

"No worries," I said. "It will be an elf dance. No one will expect you to know the steps. I'll lead."

Her smile grew. "I have a feeling you're going to lead in pretty much everything related to our *engagement*."

I'd obtain her consent, naturally, but I didn't mind leading off the dance floor as well as on.

It would be very easy to give her a child.

Would it be as easy to hold back my heart?

CHAPTER 7
KATE

The music swelled; a lilting tune that sounded incredibly foreign. A monster melody, if the musicians were anything to go by.

Tylik towered over me. Unable to put my hands around his shoulders, I could only place them on his forearms.

One of his arms went around my lower back while the other took my hand, lifting it as if we were going to waltz. But once we'd started moving, we didn't follow the box pattern I vaguely remembered playing with when I was a teenager.

We started off by taking three quick steps to my right, followed by two slower steps to the left. After a few more stilted paces to the right, we separated and gracefully glided our arms out, our fingers pointing toward the ceiling.

Tylik did this with grace. I followed his direction

with jerky movements, hoping I wasn't embarrassing him.

We repeated this pattern in the opposite direction. Our next move was a bit more complicated, and I worried I'd make him cringe with my rough attempts at this intricate dance. We joined hands and stepped toward each other, our bodies brushing together. He tapped his right heel on the floor—not in a sharp movement, but with complete elegance—followed by his left foot. I mostly did the same thing.

All the while, his "adoring" gaze remained on me. He was performing for Finni and the crowd, but I couldn't drag my attention away from the warmth in his eyes.

The music continued, and we repeated the pattern.

Elves lining the edge of the dance floor watched us with admiration, a few tapping their fingers together softly, which appeared to be the same as clapping and not a gesture of scorn.

They seemed to be buying the idea we were engaged.

As for the humans, most smiled as if this was a fairy-tale come true.

Finally, the song came to an end, and Tylik stopped, me not long after. He bowed to me and to the audience.

He moved close and lowered his head to speak by my ear. "Would it be alright to kiss you? My aunt will expect it."

My heart flipped over when it shouldn't. This would be a pretend kiss to go along with our very new, though mostly pretend engagement. "Of course."

He swept me up in his arms to bring our faces level.

I expected a quick peck, something I'd barely remember.

Instead, his hungry mouth slanted across mine. My brain spun out of control, and with a moan, I wrapped my arms around his shoulders, holding tight.

Was he lulling me? I'd heard elves could do that, lull someone and make them do things they never would on their own.

Despite my spinning brain, I felt in full control of my senses, which meant my emotions were generated solely by Tylik' kiss.

If this was a sample of what I'd experience in his bedroom, I was in deep trouble.

CHAPTER 8
TYLIK

I intended to kiss Kate only long enough to please my aunt. But when she moaned, I lost all control. I deepened our kiss, gliding my tongue across her plump lips, parting them. I wrapped my arms around her while my groin tightened, my cock jerking toward the front of my pants.

It was only when laughter boomed that I realized I was kissing Kate in front of my people and numerous humans.

When I lifted my head, I took in her limpid features and groaned. Her eyes had slid partway closed, and her lips—ripe and rosy—parted. Her eyelids opened, and she gazed at me with enough heat to make my cock ignore my inner command and continue stiffening.

"Jeez, Tylik," she said. "You pack a punch."

I had not hit her.

Oh, she meant my kiss meant something to her too.

"I . . ." What could I say? I'd intended to hold back true passion until we were alone in my bedroom. It appeared I was no more in control of my body's response to her than I was over this engagement.

I dipped my head toward her and placed her on her feet as she gazed up at me in wonder, her fingertips gently touching her swollen lips.

"Would you like to get a drink?" I asked, pushing aside the words I wanted to say, which were, *would you come to my bed tonight?*

"Sure," she said, holding out her hand. The heat had flown from her eyes, which was a good thing, but it was replaced with reservation.

The music began again as I led her off the dance floor, moving around those returning to dance.

We stopped at the drink fountain.

"Vrok," I said, dipping my head toward my friend standing nearby. Reaching out, I carefully stroked the dragonette, Merith, perched on his shoulder, admiring its golden scales. The tiny beast leaned into my hand and purred.

Vrok's gaze slid from me to Kate. "I didn't realize you two knew each other."

"It was quite sudden," Kate said, playing the role. "He swept me off my feet, as they say."

A woman scurried over to stand at Kate's other side, whispering, though I could still hear.

"What's going on?" she asked. She glanced at me, but her eyes widened when she spied Vrok.

He studiously avoided looking at her, and I understood why. Kate's friend was equally lovely, but Vrok and his fiancée had recently broken off their engagement. He'd told me he wasn't going to try with someone new. He was "finished with love," and he "wouldn't trust another woman again". I felt bad for him and hoped after time, he'd reconsider his vow.

"Tylik?" Kate said, calling my attention. "This is my best friend, Seyla. Seyla? My . . . fiancé. And this is . . ." She waved to my friend.

"Vrok," I said.

"Yes, Vrok." Kate leaned close to me. "Can I tell Seyla the truth?"

I nodded.

Her whispers continued. "He's my future baby daddy."

"I thought you didn't want more than a few quickies," Seyla hissed softly.

"My plans changed. I . . . We . . ." She must've noted my aunt approaching, because she frowned and lifted her voice for the general crowd. "It's quite sudden, isn't it?" She linked her arm through mine, though she could only reach my lower arm without a stretch that would probably be awkward. Simpering up at me, she continued, "I met Tylik weeks ago, and it was pretty much love at first sight. When he spontaneously proposed, how could I say no?"

How indeed? Actually, she'd proposed to me. Would she share that with our children?

Except she only wanted one child, then a divorce.

I was beginning to have regrets about this already, and not because I wasn't willing to give her what she asked for.

There was a good chance I could fall in love with my cute little human.

CHAPTER 9

KATE

Tylik gave us a ride home after the ball in an elf vehicle straight out of a fairytale. Creatures that looked like unicorns were hitched to the front, though they had wings and took flight as soon as we were seated.

"Why isn't the carriage dangling from the back of the unicorns?" I asked, excited about being this high off the ground.

He frowned. "They have horns and wings, but they're not unicorns."

"Do unicorns actually exist?"

"How could you believe anything else?"

Wow. I shook that idea off for now.

"They're flisteers," he said. "And a whisper of magic keeps us level."

Seyla kept peering out the window before shooting me grins and wiggling her eyebrows in his direction. I understood why. He was super-hot and super-wonderful.

I didn't have regrets about our agreement, but frankly, I was a bit nervous about moving into his place in a few days. The emotions churning inside me indicated more than a friendly respect for a guy who'd agreed to give me a baby.

The vehicle dropped onto the driveway beside the B&B, and the unicorns clop-clop-clopped up the smooth surface until they reached the walkway leading to the front porch of the big structure, where they stopped.

"Would you mind waiting here?" Tylik asked me. "We have a few things to discuss. I'll escort your friend to the door and make sure she's safely inside."

At my nod, they got out.

"See you inside," Seyla said with a wiggle of her eyebrows. "I'll wait up."

He returned not long after, sliding into the seat beside me.

"So much to do," he said.

"Off the top of my head . . ." I ticked them off in my mind. "I'll need a dress. Where will we get married and what kind of ceremony do you want?"

"My aunt will insist we use the ballroom. As for the ceremony, I like the idea of doing something completely human."

"Alright. We'll need to order flowers and book a caterer if we can find one."

"Storm's a friend. I'll ask if his restaurant can cater the event for us."

I nodded, thinking. "We'll need to pick a menu. I'll speak to Rylee about a cake."

Nervous, my swallow didn't want to go down. "I don't have a lot of money at the moment to pay for everything."

"Why would you do so?"

"It's traditional for the bride and her family to pay. My mom doesn't have any more money than me. I'm sure she'll contribute what she can, but it won't be much. It won't even cover my gown."

"You will not pay for anything."

"I can't expect you to do this."

He placed his hand on mine. "You're doing me a huge favor by not only marrying me but also teaching me about human traditions and culture. If you hadn't offered to help, I'd be forced to return to the fae realm."

Since there was just no way I could pay for all this, I didn't argue with him, though I winced. "Thank you."

"What else?"

"I'm sure there's a billion things we need to discuss. I'll carry a notepad around with me and jot them down. We can talk about it some more tomorrow if you have time to meet up."

"I do. Other than that, we need to ensure that we share the same stories," he said, raking his fingers through his golden hair. "I suggest we meet often. We can learn simple things about each other, then expand on that. During this process, I'll gain insight into human behavior."

"What sort of human activities and lingo would you like to learn?" I asked.

"Everything. Would you teach me to drive a carriage with an internal combustion engine?"

Because he sounded serious, I held back my laugh at his technical term. I waved my hand in the direction of the unicorns standing placidly, awaiting further instruction. "Why do you need to learn to drive a car when you have flisteers?"

"Driving looks incredibly fun."

I had my license, so there was no harm in being his instructor. "Driving it is, then. We'll get you a permit, and you can challenge the road."

His frown deepened. "Do your roads attack? I hadn't seen this."

"Roads don't attack, but other drivers do sometimes."

"I will arm myself then," he said gravely. "Perhaps a sword."

"No sword needed." This was going to be interesting.

"I see. Do you have time for my first lesson soon?" he asked.

"How about Wednesday? We'll need to arrange things first."

"Very well. We can meet tomorrow at the park, then again on Monday to continue our other lessons. Teach me everything you can."

"I'm off tomorrow, but I have to work on Monday. I'm done at two, however."

He nodded. "I also must work. I'll leave my place of

business, Mystic Mixtures, at clock of the two as well." He sighed. "So much to learn." His chuckle rang out. "Clock of the two is not correct. Two, as you said. By the way, I appreciate your efforts at the ball. Your savvy wits saved my awkward introduction."

"We should've thought of names before we left the library." I smacked my forehead with my palm. "I can't believe I didn't introduce myself to you when we were alone." I lowered my voice, mocking myself. "Hey, hot elf guy, how about we get married? And by the way, would you also give me a baby?"

His head tilted, and he watched my face in the light from streetlamps. "You think I have heat?"

"Hot means attractive."

His face cleared. "Oh, yes, this I understand. You are also well-heated."

I snickered. "Thanks." I pressed my fingers over my lips, still chuckling. "I should probably hold comments like that back." Actually, I had to stop thinking like that too.

"Actually, you should not."

My laughter slowed. Our conversation suddenly felt serious, and while my heart was hopping around in my chest in excitement, he didn't mean anything by his comment. We were doing this to make sure he could remain in Monsterville.

We weren't falling in love.

"As for my driving lesson, I will also need to procure an internal combustion engine-powered vehicle. I'll have it delivered here as soon as possible."

We'd need to go to the DMV before hopping on the road. "Do you have identification?"

"I was gifted such a thing when I first arrived here."

We'd have to see what the DMV said about that. I assumed they'd already been through this before. Goreg drove, as did Raze, the ogre living with his girlfriend Elisa in the back of Goreg's converted barn.

"What details do you want to know about me?" I asked. "We could go through a few things right now, then more tomorrow."

We exchanged the basics. He had a younger sister who preferred to live in the fae realm, the one he hoped would take the duchess title so he could avoid becoming a duke. Their parents died after a freak witch spell when he was three and her only one. Finni raised them. No wonder he adored his aunt so much.

He owned an alchemy shop where he sold various ingredients for spells, which was totally cool.

"What kind of spells are we talking about?" I asked.

"Simple ones. Forget-me spells or ones to make a woman extra fertile."

"Nothing to make someone fall in love, right?"

"I suppose someone could craft such a spell if they wanted to, but castings like that are forbidden according to the treaty we agreed upon when we joined human society. We swore in blood. No one would risk breaking their word."

"What would happen if they did?"

"You're aware of our demon sheriff."

"Venom," I said. "I've heard about him, but I haven't met him yet. He's not a real demon, is he?"

"He was cast from the underworld."

"How does something like that happen?"

Tylik shrugged. "I don't know why he was banished, but he must've done something wrong. You could ask Venom."

I chuckled. "No thanks. I'm not tangling with a demon sheriff."

"I thought the underworld was kinda like hell."

"Kinda." He flashed a smile. "See? I'm learning human terms. Kind-a and that I have heat." He patted his chest.

Damn, he was cute. "I'll teach you some more."

He dipped his head forward in a bow. "This, I appreciate greatly."

I liked that I could do something for him. I didn't want whatever we had between us to be solely about sex.

I wanted to be his friend.

"Tell me more about you," he said.

It was flattering to have the attention of such a gorgeous guy, even if he asked only because he needed the information.

I told him about growing up without siblings, that my mom raised me.

"And your father?"

"He took off when I was little."

"I'm sorry," he said.

I shrugged. "They squabbled all the time. I don't blame him for bailing."

"Bail . . .?"

"Leave us."

"He squabbled with your mother, as you say, but he didn't just *bail* on her, but you as well. I doubt you did anything to make him eager to leave."

"It's hard to say." And I'd rather not talk about my dad. "My mom was enough."

He nodded. "Where do you work?"

"Rylee's bakery. I run the cash register and serve customers."

"You didn't go to college?"

"There was no money for anything like that."

His face took on a solemn cast. Emotions I couldn't understand swirled inside me, but I wanted him to like and respect me, not feel pity.

"What are your favorite foods?" I asked, driving this convo away from poor Kate who didn't have prospects before she met an almost-duke elf.

We shared more before growing silent. It was hard to believe we'd run out of things to talk about already, but I guess that's what happened on first dates, assuming that's what we could call this.

"I'll walk with you to the door," he finally said.

We strolled up the drive and took the stairs to the front door, pausing beside it.

"Thank you," I said. I felt I needed to say it. He was changing my life in so many ways, and I felt nothing but gratitude.

"Thank *you*," he said. "Without you, I wouldn't have a chance of remaining in this fascinating realm."

I hated the thought of him leaving forever. He had an almost childlike wonder of our world, and I was looking forward to showing him the best parts of it.

"I should go in," I said as we stood on the front porch.

He teased a curl dangling across my shoulder. "I'll see you tomorrow?"

I nodded and started to turn away, but he snagged my arm and tugged me back around to face him.

"One more kiss," he said, his voice deep and husky. "If you will permit this."

"I will."

For one second, I thought he'd asked because he truly wanted to kiss me. Until I reminded myself that he wanted to kiss me in case anyone was watching. For all I knew, the unicorns could talk and were spies.

It didn't matter why. I'd enjoyed his first kiss.

I wanted another.

CHAPTER 10
TYLIK

The next day, we met up at the park. I noted Kate walked and didn't ride in a carriage.

"Where's your internal combustion engine transportation?" I asked the second she joined me.

"I don't have one. My legs work great, though." She grinned up at me, her cheeks pink, and her hair floating around her face like beams of a sunset streaking across the sky. I was stunned by how beautiful she was.

With a shake of my head, I forced my mind to function.

"A friend has offered to help me obtain a vehicle," I said. Max would take me later today.

"You won't steal it, will you?" At my frown, she snickered. "Kidding."

I grinned, appreciating her humor. "The vehicle will be delivered to your home soon. Once you've taught me how to maneuver it about town, you'll keep it. I'll procure a second."

"You want to give me a car?" she gulped. "Why?"

"Because you need it."

"I assume I can't ride around in your unicorn carriage."

I sensed irony in her words, but her smooth face suggested she was being completely serious. "I could assign a carriage to you if you'd prefer."

"Tylik." Warning came through in her voice. "I don't need a vehicle."

I lifted my eyebrows. "How else will you teach me?"

"Hey, it's Tylik and Kate," someone said from behind me. A glance over my shoulder revealed Rylee and Gunner striding our way with their small son, Josh, trotting beside them.

I stooped down and held out my arms, and Josh squealed and ran to me, leaping at the last moment. I scooped him up and spun him around, and he squealed some more while I whispered against his neck.

Finally, I put him down, and he leaned against my leg, gazing up at me.

Rylee joined us, shaking her head. "You've created a monster."

Stroking the boy's shoulder, I frowned. "I believe you and Gunner created this monster."

"You know what I mean."

I wasn't completely sure I did, but nuance was another human thing I needed to learn.

"When Kate mentioned you two were meeting here," Rylee said, "it reminded me of how much Josh loves coming to the park. I have to pry him off the swings at the end of the day." She winked at Kate. "As for you two, I can't believe you kept your relationship secret all this time."

I cleared my throat and shot Kate a look of gratitude for maintaining the ruse even with Rylee. "You know how it is. My aunt is a powerful female. If anyone heard before we were ready to make our announcement, they'd hound us both." Something I needed to take care of. I nodded to Kate. "I'll ensure you're assigned someone to protect you as soon as possible."

"Why?" she asked, blinking up at me.

"Someone might kidnap you," Rylee said with a heavy sigh. "Hold you for ransom."

"You're . . . You work at an apothecary," Kate said. "I know you could be a duke if you agreed, but you're just an everyday elf, right?"

"Not quite," I said. "My family has considerable power within the fae realm."

"Venom would make a perfect bodyguard," Rylee said. "But I imagine he's busy. Who'd mess with a demon?"

"I don't need a bodyguard," Kate said with a huff.

"Vrok recently opened a security business," I said. I should've thought of this last night at the ball and asked him.

"He'll be perfect," Rylee said.

"Guys," Kate said. She rolled her eyes. "I don't need a bodyguard, but if you insist, anyone will do. My new bodyguard can drive Tylik's car."

"*Your* car," I said.

She rolled her eyes again. My fiancée was incredibly sweet. Somehow, knowing we'd soon be intimate made her even more appealing. I'd noticed her right away when she entered the ballroom of course. Meeting her had only strengthened my interest.

"Have you met Vrok?" Rylee asked, nudging Kate's arm. "He has dark green skin, black hair, and to die for muscles."

"He looks like every other orc," Gunner said with a laugh, not displaying a bit of jealousy about his wife gushing over a different monster.

"I met him last night at the ball," Kate said. "Are you sure I need a bodyguard?"

I loved her fire and how she spoke up for herself, but she needed someone to watch over her when I wasn't around. In the elf kingdom, it was common for the aristocracy to juggle for power, and some could be quite ruthless. And since internal combustion engine drivers could be dangerous, it would be wise to ensure my fiancée was well-protected.

"I guess we should get going and leave you two alone," Rylee said with a wink. She took Gunner's hand. "Ready to continue our walk, love?"

He leaned over and kissed her.

"Bye, Kate. Bye, Tylik," Josh chirped, looking up at me.

I lifted him and spun him around once more while he giggled before returning him to the ground. He skipped after his parents, pausing to turn back and wave.

"You're going to make a great dad," Kate said.

"Josh is amazing. So much fun."

She studied me before returning her gaze to our friends. "They're happy together." A touch of longing lingered in her voice.

She'd made it clear she didn't want a permanent relationship, and I'd agreed to respect her wishes. But now that I was getting to know her better—and we'd shared some amazing kisses—I was having regrets.

Would it be wrong of me to try to change her mind about sharing a future with me?

We strolled through the park, sharing bits about our lives and picking the menu for the reception, which I'd pass onto Storm, who'd agreed to cater the event.

Kate loved seafood, which I wasn't fond of. She'd always dreamed of going hang gliding. I wasn't sure what that could be, but if she wanted to do it, I'd find a way.

"Seyla's taking me gown shopping on Thursday; it's the soonest we could get an appointment."

"I understand if I see you in your gown before the wedding, we'll be cursed with seven years of bad luck, so please don't show me once you've selected your dress."

A frown filled her face. "I haven't heard of that, but . . ." Her expression cleared. "Oh, you mean seven years bad luck if you break a mirror. We'll avoid that as well. I've heard of not showing the groom the gown until he sees her walking down the aisle, however."

I cleared the huskiness from my throat. "I am very much looking forward to seeing you in your gown on our wedding day."

CHAPTER 11

TYLIK

We met at the park again on Monday after work. In addition to serving customers at Mystic Mixtures, I'd made arrangements for the procurement of an internal combustion engine vehicle.

Paying anything but gold for such a thing confused me. In the fae realm, coins were exchanged for items. In the human realm, one must sit while a male discussed extended warranties and asked if I wished to apply a coat to the underside of the carriage. Why would an object crafted from metal need to wear a coat?

Finally, I was able to complete the transaction. It would arrive at her place of residence soon.

As Kate walked toward me, she carried a white box. Her other hand lifted to wave. I stared in wonder as usual. Everything about her tugged on my heart, from her kindness to me, to her warm smile, and the way she thought of others before herself.

"I stopped by Rylee's bakery to buy a cupcake, but

Rylee bustled from the back and handed me this box," she said. "She told me not to open it until I was with you. She said it's a sample of the wedding cake she'll be making for us."

"I can't wait to see."

We sat at a picnic table, and Kate placed the box between us.

"My aunt's hosting a dinner party in our honor Friday night," I said.

"That's nice of her."

"I researched and discovered it's traditional in some human societies for the groom's family to host such a meal. Usually it follows a rehearsal of the wedding, though we won't be doing that."

"I don't imagine we need to practice."

We would marry regardless.

"Will your aunt's dinner be a long or short event?" Kate asked, fiddling with a corner of the box.

"We can leave once dinner has concluded, and we've shared the usual social niceties. There won't be dancing afterward, if that's of concern," I added. "The only other expectation will be sitting with my aunt and a few others in one of the parlors before the meal commences. She's been gushing about you since you two met, and she wants to get to know you better."

"Alright. Sure," Kate said. "I'll be happy to have dinner with her and a few guests."

"Thank you."

She tugged away a plastic knife secured to the top of

the box and lifted the lid. "Oh," she cried out, pointing the knife. "Rylee crafted an elf and a human on the top. It's like a mini wedding cake featuring you and me. She's so clever."

"It's almost a shame to cut it."

"Right?"

Slicing the cupcake in half revealed its white center. Chocolate frosting topped it, covered with colorful glittering specks, and the intricate picture of us.

I was touched. Honored. I'd reach out to her tonight to thank her.

"And now you've given us a divorce," I said in a droll voice, trying not to laugh.

She stared at me for a long moment, perhaps trying to determine if I was serious before she her laugh choked out.

"I could put us through counseling and get us back together if you'd like," she said, hoisting the two halves up until they met again. "There we are; a couple once more. But really, let's try it."

I studied her face, but I still couldn't quite tell what she was thinking. Studiously avoiding my gaze, she busied laying a napkin in front of us and placing half of the cupcake on each.

"Fork?" I asked.

She blinked. "It's finger food."

"It's cake. One eats cake with a fork."

"Nah, fingers work just as well. Let's practice." She broke off a piece of hers and held it out to me.

I pinned my eyes on it. "Practice what?"

"At the reception, we'll cut the cake, and I'll feed you a piece. Then you'll feed me."

"What's the meaning of this ritual?"

"It symbolizes a mutual promise to provide for each other."

"Then I'll gladly eat this cake," I said gravely.

"Sometimes, people smoosh it in the other person's face, but I'd rather we didn't do that."

"I'd never smoosh cake in your face," I said with horror. "That would be disrespectful."

She laughed again. "I've wondered how those relationships turn out when they begin their marriage doing something like that."

"If their cake is on their face and not in their belly, it defeats the purpose of showing the other you will provide for them."

"Exactly." She nudged the bite of cake toward me. "Try it."

I held her wrist and carefully ate the bite, making sure I slid my tongue across her fingertip.

She sucked in a breath and stared at me, bemused. As I ate the bite, I kept my gaze locked on hers. Once I'd swallowed, I licked the frosting off each of her fingers.

"Talk about making me swoon," she breathed. "I'm going to melt and slide off the bench. Puddle Kate, they'll call me."

"I like making you melt."

"I'm sure you do," she said dryly, though she shot me a smile.

"Allow me to feed you. As you said, we must practice traditions like this to ensure we do not make mistakes."

I broke off a piece of my own cupcake and held it out to her. She must read the dare in my eyes because she held my wrist.

Leaning close, she took the bite from me, and just like I'd done with her, she didn't let go. After swallowing, she sucked on each of my fingers, making sure to flick her tongue across the tips.

I sucked in a breath and watched her.

"You're dangerous, Kate," I said in a voice gone very husky. "There are things . . ." I shook my head.

"What were you going to say?" She released my hand.

"There are many things we could lick."

Her pupils widened. "Perhaps, like feeding each other cake, it's something we need to practice?"

"Do you mean that?"

"I do."

Ohhh.

"I have a question," I said.

She nodded, her lips separating in anticipation.

"Would you . . .?"

She tilted her head, an inviting smile teasing her lips upward. "What?"

"I'd like to show you where I live." I was ready to bare myself to her. How would she feel if she knew how vulnerable I was to her already? "I know you won't move in with me for a few days, but I'd like to share my home with you today."

"You don't live at Finni's estate?"

"I'd only do that if I had to," I said. My aunt had insisted at first, but I'd persuaded her I was safe enough in my own home. "It's much too elegant. I'm a simple male."

"In addition to being an almost duke."

"And that is why you'll turn me into an almost-human instead, my lovely fiancée. Then the line can be passed to my sister. I've shrugged off the mantle, and I have no interest in picking it up."

She held out her hand. "Show me where the real Tylik lives, then," she said with excitement. "I can't wait to see."

Trepidation skidded through me. Would she like my home? It would be hers as well until we parted.

I was beginning to believe I didn't want that day to arrive.

We packed up the rest of the cupcake and took it with us, walking to my carriage. The flisteers stomped their feet as we climbed inside. They took wing, and it didn't take long to reach the long drive to my somewhat secluded home. The beasts landed and plodded along the crushed stone.

"Lots of trees," she said, peering out her window. "It's pretty, though." She pointed out my side. "Look, deer."

They scattered, darting into the woods when they spied the flisteers.

The carriage rounded a bend and emerged from the

forest into a big open meadow where I'd had my home constructed.

Kate gasped and pressed her fingers against her lips. "Wait. You haven't been here long enough to build something like this. Did you buy it?"

"When the realm opened, allowing some of us to cross over, I hired Max and urged him to rush to complete it."

The flisteers came to a halt, and I wanted to see if she liked it or if she'd reject it—and pretty much me.

She turned bright eyes my way. "It's so pretty. It looks like a hobbit house."

CHAPTER 12

KATE

"This place is incredible," I exclaimed as I got out of the car. I gazed in awe at the rounded structure sheltered by the forest behind. Wildflowers filled the meadow, a carpet of every color imaginable.

The exterior walls had been constructed of a mixture of stone and wood, and they formed a beautiful mosaic, ranging from earthy browns to dark greens. The roof was covered with thatch, giving it an inviting, cozy feel. A stone chimney jutted out of the top, though no smoke coiled from it.

The windows were round and good sized, and a large, carved wooden door invited me to step closer.

"Does a horbet mean it is unappealing?" Tylik asked, concern taking over his features.

"The Hobbits were characters from a movie, Lord of the Rings. They were a peaceful, simple race."

"Am I copying them?"

"You're not one, but anyone can build a similar structure. As an elf, I'm confident you can get away with it."

"Then I'm relieved. I like it. It's very appealing."

After we left the carriage, the unicorns took flight, soaring over the forest and out of view.

"Do you call them when you need them?" I asked.

"Don't humans do this with their internal combustion engines?"

"Not quite." Teaching him to drive was going to be a lot of fun.

We walked up the path made of cobblestones, me pausing to exclaim about the gorgeous flowerbeds lining the sides.

"Who did all this?" I asked.

"Would you believe I did much of the landscaping myself?"

"It's gorgeous."

He dipped his head in thanks.

We reached the front door, and I traced my fingers along the intricate carving. "This too?"

"Yes."

"You're an artist, aren't you?"

He winced. "My sister teases me about my craft."

"Why?"

"It's boring."

"Not to me."

His gaze probed me. What did he see? "Do you like art?"

"I don't know much about it, but I'd love to learn. Would you show me what you like and tell me why?"

"I will." His voice came out so light and happy it made my heart soar.

I couldn't seem to hold myself back. I liked him. And while liking him was okay—we were going to have sex and get married—I liked him in a way that could turn into something that might leave me shattered.

"Would you like to see the inside of our home?" he asked, his eyes gleaming with eagerness.

Our home. Why didn't the thought of sharing this place with him scare me?

"I'd love to," I said.

He placed his hand near the door, and a click rang out. "A bit of magic allowed in this world. I'll teach it your touch when you move in." He nudged the door open and swept his hand out for me to enter ahead of him.

I stepped into a cozy entryway and paused, taking in the simple stairs on the opposite side of the room leading up to an open loft with a rail spanning either side.

"I sit up there and contemplate things," he said with a laugh.

"Have you drawn any conclusions yet?"

His gaze shot to me. "I suspect I'm close."

Heat rose into my face. He couldn't be speaking of me. "Maybe you'll share your thoughts sometime."

"I think I'll eventually have to." With a nod to his right, he led me into a good-sized living room.

"It's so spacious and inviting." I looked around with a grin, feeling like I'd stepped into one of my favorite movies. Crossing the room, I stood near the large fireplace built into the outer wall, unlit but still giving off a sense of comfort.

"I designed the fireplace," he said. "Urging the builders to use the same stones as the walls. I wanted to give my home a natural, earthy feel."

"It's amazing." I couldn't stop smiling as I took it all in. Built in a timber frame design, he'd used simple white walls in between. The rough-hewn beams had to be eight inches across, and I couldn't imagine where he'd found the trees.

"I had each beam cut through sustainable means, ensuring the construction crew carefully selected trees on land I own high in the mountains. It had to be kiln-dried, of course, or it would split. I've planted three times the number to replace those selected. A few had early disease, while others were so big, they consumed more than their share of the available resources, preventing younger trees from thriving."

"I love that you thought of the trees before you cut them." Few others would. They'd go in with big equipment and slice through everything, leaving devastation behind.

"Your trees don't communicate like ours, but it is still important to respect ancient ones."

I studied the painting hanging above the fireplace depicting what must be a scene from the fae realm. Sunlight dappled the lush forest, and a small cabin nestled among the trees. Wherever I looked, I picked out more amazing details.

He joined me, placing his hands on my shoulders

from behind. I liked how he held me, as if he treasured me more than anything else. It gave me a heady feeling.

"See the sprites?" he asked, pointing to the bright flowers scattered across the forest floor.

I had to squint before I picked them out, and I sucked in my breath. "They're tiny. And now that you've shown them to me, I see other hidden things, like small insects with bright little faces, clouds scattering across the sky in patterns that reveal leaping deer and soaring birds, plus the face in the tree in the center that at first glance looks like swirling bark."

"He's a friendly tree, but I couldn't get him to smile."

Amazed, I glanced up at him. "You painted this?"

He nodded. "It's one I actually like."

"I suspect you do more than contemplation on your loft."

"I have a small studio there."

"Have you thought of selling your art?" I asked.

"Who'd buy it?"

"I would." I'd have to save for months to afford something like this, but it was as magical as Tylik. "You're more than just an herbal apothecary."

He grinned. "Don't forget. I'm an almost-duke."

"Who doesn't want the title?"

"Would you?"

"Nope. I'm a simple person, and I'm happy that way."

"Imagine growing up with royalty all around you, along with backbiting and many who'd do anything— even commit murder—to gain a favor."

"Money's not everything."

"Neither is power."

I studied the painting again, picking out more details, before he took my hand and urged me across the living room.

"Let me show you the rest of the place," he said. Inside his own home, he seemed relaxed, as if he'd shed the constraints placed on him in the fae realm.

He took me upstairs, watching as I strolled around his loft, shifting the cozy rocker by the rail where he must sit and read a book or look out the front windows.

I stopped at the easel with a rough drawing of a woman who looked vaguely familiar. My breath caught. "That's me."

He shot me a nervous smile. "I hope you don't mind that I plan to paint you. I started this last night."

"What am I doing here?" I pointed to the area beneath me on the canvas. "I'm lounging on something."

"I thought I'd set you in the fae realm. I realize few humans are allowed to travel there, but I could picture how much you'd enjoy it."

"I can't imagine going to a place like that," I said. "Can you feel magic everywhere?"

"It floats across your skin. You breathe it in and release it until you don't know where you stop and it begins."

"How could you give that up to live here?"

"I like it here. The fae and elves are . . . flighty? I'm not sure how else to name it. And too often manipulative."

"So are many humans."

"Here, however, I feel like I can see it before it smacks

me in the head. Humans feel more alive, perhaps because their lifespans are shorter than ours. In comparison, we feel dull. I'm not sure how to explain it."

"How long will you live?" This was something I hadn't considered.

"No longer than a human. Without magic, we age like everyone else in your realm."

Interesting. "And you'd give up living almost forever to be here?"

He shot me a soft smile. "I already have."

We went downstairs, and he took me to a room on the right after the living room.

"My place is small," he said. "Only one bedroom, but I like it that way. If I want to expand, I could add another room on the back or finish the loft."

"And lose your contemplation space? Nah," I said with a laugh.

"I do enjoy sitting there. Painting there. I find it relaxing." He waved to his bedroom. "This room's self-explanatory."

The bedframe had been handmade from thick pieces of wood, carefully etched and polished to perfection. It was huge and flanked by side tables. A bureau sat between two windows at the foot of the bed, and I crossed the room to look outside, taking in the dense forest about thirty feet away, plus a firepit with wooden furniture placed around it.

"My outdoor cooking station," he said, pointing to a structure on the right. "I understand this is a human thing. This Q of the barb."

"Barbecue?"

"Yes, that. I asked Max to construct what most humans use. I haven't tried it, but I hope to soon. We can sizzle the cats."

"Excuse me?" I barked.

He frowned. "Not cats. *Dogs*."

"We're not sizzling either of them." My chuckle rang out. "I think you mean hot dogs, which are not made from dogs."

"I hoped not. I do enjoy pets."

"We could grill, or sizzle, as you say, burgers sometime."

"What is a burger made from?"

"A cow. Or turkey meat if you prefer. There are vegetable alternatives too."

"We will try them all."

He'd had a roof built over his grill to keep out the rain.

"Is that honeysuckle growing over the top?" I asked.

"It will smell amazing in the summer."

"I really love your home." I turned back to the bedroom. A thick green oval rug covered part of the wide-plank wooden floor, and it matched the bedspread.

"I built my own bed," he said, gesturing toward it.

"You've been awfully busy over the past month," I said.

"I kept picturing myself sharing this with someone, but I assumed it would be a pet who I would not eat."

It was too easy to see him resting beneath the blankets, me lying with him. Could he see the same thing?

This relationship was too new for stuff like that, but my body had a mind of its own. My core throbbed, and if he took my hand and led me to the bed, I wouldn't refuse him.

I stared at the bed, unable to drag myself away.

Again, he joined me, standing behind me with his hands on my shoulders. If I wanted, I could lean against him, and it would almost be like he was embracing me.

Before I could talk myself out of it, I sunk into him, savoring his warmth and that bit of magic he still possessed that slid across my skin with a touch lighter than a feather.

He turned me in his arms, and I sought his eyes, unsure what I'd find there.

Desire.

When I didn't pull away, he lowered his head, and his mouth claimed mine.

CHAPTER 13

TYLIK

With each room I showed her, it became easier to picture Kate living here with me. I'd paint in the evening, and she'd sit in the rocker, suggesting colors I'd use because I sensed she had a good eye. Maybe even lifting a brush to a canvas herself.

I could also imagine her cradling our child in her arms. I'd pause in my painting to go stand beside her, gazing down at the beautiful picture of my wife and the child we'd created.

A longing for this life shot through me, though it wasn't unexpected.

This was an arrangement to get my aunt to release me from my inheritance, but I couldn't drive the images from my mind.

The ache for something I'd never dreamed of until I met Kate combined with my sadness that it would never come true.

When I put my hands on her shoulders, I didn't

expect her to lean into me, to seek the warmth of my body and the shelter of my arms.

Then she turned and looked up at me, and for a moment, the feelings coursing through me were revealed on *her* face. She said she only wanted a baby, that she didn't need love or someone by her side. I couldn't imagine why she didn't want love, and I'd never force her to care for me.

I still couldn't resist touching her.

When her lips parted, I kissed her.

Her arms went around my shoulders like they belonged there.

She moaned and stepped backward. Her hands fisted my clothing, taking me with her. We tumbled onto the bed; me landing on top of her.

A groan ripped through her.

Thinking I'd hurt her, I started to rise.

"No," she cried, tightening her grip on my shirt.

I'd give almost anything to love her body.

I eased to the side and kissed her some more, enjoying the feel of her mouth beneath mine.

She wore a skirt and top, and as I stroked my tongue across hers, coiling them together, I traced my fingers up her thigh.

Her legs parted, and I sought between them, finding her wet through her undergarment.

She lifted her hips, and I slid them off her, tossing them aside.

I trailed kisses along her neck, and she clung to me as if I was all she'd ever need. I couldn't imagine being someone's everything, but for this moment, I'd be Kate's.

When I slid my fingers under her shirt and cupped her breast, I found her firm nipple. A groan shot through me.

She tugged her bra and shirt up, and I captured her ripe bud, running the tip of my tongue across it while gliding a finger through the wet folds between her legs.

I sucked on her nipple and found her clit, rolling it while she moaned and bucked up to meet my hand.

She was so responsive; I was going to come from the sounds she made. My cock was stiffer than it had ever been in my life, and there wasn't anything I wouldn't give to sink it deep within her, to drive myself into her until she screamed my name.

Soon, I promised myself. She'd be mine within days, and with our goal to give her a baby, I'd love her every chance I could.

I only hoped I didn't burn out completely when she told me she no longer needed me.

That was for the future. Now was for my fingers sliding into her wet passage to stroke her inner walls, for savoring her cries of pleasure.

With my thumb on her clit, her pulse point, I pumped my fingers inside her.

She moaned and urged me on, clinging to my hair while I sucked her nipple and loved her with my fingers.

There'd be no baby from this, but I didn't care. All that mattered was showing her the joy of giving in to my touch.

When she came, her entire body shuddered. I lifted my head, releasing her nipple with a wet pop, and our gazes locked.

And that was when I knew I wanted everything from Kate.

CHAPTER 14
KATE

Before I could leave for work on Tuesday, Rylee called.

"Kate, I was thinking," she said. "You're getting married in just a few days."

So many things left to do to ensure we were ready.

"Why don't you take the rest of this week off, plus next week?" Rylee said. "My treat. Consider it a wedding gift."

"You'll pay me for all that time off?" She was generous, but this was too much.

"Exactly. Enjoy making your wedding plans without stressing about coming to work."

"Are you sure?"

"Totally."

"Well, thank you. You're amazing. I really appreciate it."

"Of course. Have fun. You know I would." Her chuckle rang out.

I hung up and slouched on my bed. "Rylee is such a nice person. I can't believe she did that."

Now that my day was free, I could tackle some of the things on our list.

First, I needed to call my mom. I was moving in with Tylik on Thursday, and it was only fair I let her know what was going on.

"Hey," I said when she picked up.

"Oh, Kate, honey! So glad you called. I haven't heard from you in a while. Is everything going okay?"

"It is. Sorry I haven't called. I've been busy."

"Is it scary living around so many monsters?" she asked in a hushed voice.

"It's wonderful."

"I can't imagine. There aren't many monsters in Chicago. Not yet anyway."

"If some move there, be nice to them, okay?" I said.

"Of course I will. You know me. I'm not mean to anyone."

This was true. My mom was generous to a fault, volunteering at the food kitchen and the local animal shelter. Because she had MS and needed canes to get around, she worked as a receptionist at a doctor's office. Throughout my life, she'd worked incredibly hard and shared whatever we didn't need.

"Why did you call?" she asked.

"First, I'll send you some money. I've got a good job, and I'm making more than I need." Not really, but she needed it more than me. Sometimes, she had to skip work on days when the pain was too severe. The co-pay for her medicine cost a fortune, but she had to have it when her body tried to slide out of remission.

"Don't do that, honey," she said. "I'm doing fine. But if you have any to spare, the animal shelter really needs pee pads and litter."

I adored how generous she was with everyone, but I wished she'd hold back a bit for herself.

"Will one hundred be enough?" It was all I could spare.

"More than enough." Her voice lowered, and her sad sigh drifted between us. "I hate that I can't send *you* money, that you always have to help me."

"I love you, Mom," I choked out. "I'm always happy to help."

Maybe it was a mistake for me to move here with Seyla. If I was in Chicago, I could be there for my mom, though she often refused my assistance. Money for animals or those in great need, yes, but rarely for herself.

But when Seyla proposed the idea, Mom insisted, stating it was time I ventured out on my own instead of hanging back all the time to be with my mother.

"Maybe you could move here," I said.

"Oh, I couldn't. I don't mind the monsters; it's not that. But I have a life here. Friends and all the good things that need doing."

It was worth a try. "I love you, Mom."

"Love you too, honey."

"I'm engaged." There was no other way to tell her than to spit it out.

"Oh . . ."

I could read her surprise from her voice, so I rushed to fill in the gaps. "His name's Tylik. We met, and it was sudden, and—"

"Tell me about him."

"He's wonderful. Kind and cute, and he's so tall. He runs an apothecary, a kind of herbal spell store for those who do magic."

"Is he a witch?"

"No, he's an elf."

"Like in that movie you watched all the time?" she asked with a sweet chuckle.

"Lord of the Rings, and yes. He looks a lot like one of the elves."

"Does he love you? Does he promise to make you happy?"

I didn't have the heart to tell her no. "I'll make sure he does." He'd give me a baby, and that would make me very happy.

I had no intention of telling her why we were getting married, nor who he was among the elf community.

"He's a good guy," I added. "I called to invite you to the wedding. I can send you extra for the bus."

"Aw, that would be wonderful. When is it?"

"Next Saturday."

"So soon? I didn't realize you were dating anyone," she said.

"We didn't want to wait any longer. It's going to be a beautiful wedding. I hope you can be here to share my special day with me."

A long pause was followed by her second sigh.

"We're holding a huge fundraiser at the shelter this Saturday."

"Oh, yes, I can see why you might not be able to make my wedding, then." Damn, my chest hurt. "I'm sorry it's such short notice."

A long pause followed.

"I'm really sorry, honey," she said. "This fundraiser is only held once a year. The animals need me desperately."

What about your daughter?

I hated feeling as if it was me or them, though. This had been my life since the time I was little; I couldn't expect her to change because I made sudden plans.

"I wish I could be there," she said softly. "Truly. But I'll be there in my heart. Know that, honey."

"Okay, Mom. I have to go."

We hung up. I tossed my phone on my bed and cupped my face, trying not to cry.

My door opened, and Seyla jumped into the room, her arms splayed out wide. "Grab your purse, girly. We're going shopping." When I didn't say anything, her smile fell. "Aw, honey. What's wrong?" She dropped onto the bed beside me and gave me a hug.

I wouldn't tell her why I was upset. She knew my mom. She knew Mom was incredibly busy. Seyla and I had been friends since we were five. She'd been the one to cheer me on the year I played field hockey when Mom was too busy to come to the games. Seyla held my hand when my first boyfriend broke up with me.

Perhaps that was why it had been easy to move away. My mom didn't truly need me, but I needed Seyla.

"I have a bottle of wine I was saving for a big occasion," she said. "But there's no time like the present. We can pour glasses and sit on the porch while we drink it. Please." Her voice croaked. "What can I do to cheer you up? Wine or would retail therapy help?"

"I really shouldn't spend any money." Not when I had to send Mom a hundred.

"You need some new clothes. I need to buy them for you."

"No, Seyla. You buy me too much already."

"Who else will I spend it on?" She lifted my chin, making me meet her eyes. "I have more than I can spend in a lifetime. Why not share it with you? You're my best friend. Let me help?"

This felt too much like me with my mom, only I was Seyla's charity. Although that wasn't completely true. Seyla cared for me, and she knew I didn't have much.

"You'll be going to fancy dinner parties," she said, injecting a known lure into her voice. "You look fabulous in worn jeans and a t-shirt, but why not gorgeous dresses instead? Can I get you a few things? We'll look for bargains."

"You say that every time, then sneak a bunch of full-priced items into my bag."

"Caught." She shrugged. "I can't help it. You're my best friend, and I love you. Let's scoot into town. There's a cute place run by a phoenix we could check out." She held up her hand. "No pressure, but if we find a few cute things that are perfect for you, I want to get them for you. My treat. Consider it a wedding gift."

"You're already buying my wedding gown as a gift, which is way too generous."

"Consider the other dresses part of your trousseau. You'll need one of those, right?"

I wasn't exactly sure what a trousseau was, but sometimes, there was no dissuading Seyla. It was better to ride along with whatever she wanted to do and smile.

"I saw a few dresses in the window that will look amazing on you." She slid off the bed and kicked off her pink slippers. "Yes? No?"

"Okay," I sighed.

"Yay. Let me throw on something vaguely more decent, and we'll skip all the way to town." Something we hadn't done since we were twelve, but it had been so much fun back then.

Maybe I needed to let skipping back into my life.

"I feel strange buying clothing and wedding stuff when I can't afford to live anywhere but at a B&B," I said. "This place is amazing, and Violet and Goreg are awesome hosts, but it's not exactly a place of my own." I kept thinking of Tylik's hobbit house and how cozy it was there. Never in my wildest dreams did I imagine I'd live in a place like that.

"Just a few dresses."

I drooled at the thought of buying pretty clothing that would make me feel good when I wore them. It was going to be hard enough to lift my head at Finni's estate with all those gorgeous fae beings sauntering around.

"Auntie to the rescue," Seyla added.

"You're younger than me, *Auntie*." I rolled my eyes. "I can't keep letting you buy things for me."

"Since you might one day be a duchess, you deserve to be dressed like a queen."

"Tylik's not a duke. He's . . . I suppose you could call him an herbal pharmacist."

"His aunt's a duchess. He's her heir, even if he doesn't want the title." She stuffed my feet into sneakers, double knotting them like I was a little kid. Snagging my jacket off the chair, she put that on me too. After she zipped it, I expected her to tap me on the nose, but thankfully, she didn't. "Let's go, sugar butt."

"Jeez, Seyla," I said as she dragged me from the room. I might protest, but I was grinning. She was my fairy godmother, and I'd never been one to turn down a shopping trip. I'd bake her cookies. She loved my pumpkin chocolate chip.

It was quiet downstairs.

"Where is everyone?" Seyla asked, tiptoeing across the front hall.

"Uncle Bub mentioned earlier that he and Grannie Vi were going out on a brunch date. I assume they've already left. The other guests must be at work."

Seyla poked her head into the parlor. "No Goreg or Violet. Maybe they're outside? Violet loves to garden. She has the magic touch."

We stepped outside to find them standing in the driveway beside a shiny red SUV, talking to a big, burly, green-skinned orc—though all of them were big, burly, and green-skinned. He wore snug black pants and an equally black button-up shirt. At first, and with his back to us, I couldn't tell who he was.

Until I spied the cute little dragonette perched on his shoulder.

Seyla paused, turning wide eyes my way. "It's Vrok." She ran her fingers through her hair and smoothed her shirt. "I'm a wreck. Why am I a wreck? I should've worn something nicer."

"You look fine." Beautiful, in fact, like always.

Vrok glanced our way, and his gaze froze on my friend. He took in Seyla striding toward him, but rather than step forward to meet her with a besotted look on his face like every other guy, he turned his back to her.

She stopped on the walk, frowning. "What's up with him?"

A very good question. "No clue."

Saying nothing, she went with me to join the others.

"There you are," Goreg said. He dipped his head forward. "Wellisteer aradesc."

I returned the gargoyle phrase for well wishes, taking in our gargoyle landlord who held his wife's hand. They were so cute together, it made me swoon. His wing rested protectively across her back, and despite following along with the conversation, she kept looking up at him with complete adoration. Her baby bump was just as cute. They expected their first child around Christmas, and I couldn't wait to see if their baby had Goreg's gorgeous stony skin and wings or her almost white-blonde hair. Maybe a bit of both.

Violet's little sister, Halle, rode her bicycle up and

down the drive, singing a tune about monsters and flowers.

"I don't know if you've met Vrok yet, Kate," Goreg said. "Tylik sent him."

"We actually did," Seyla said, leaning into me for emotional support. "At the ball." While guys might flock around Seyla, she barely noticed any of them. But she remembered Vrok, which said he meant something to her. Him showing no interest must hurt.

"Tylik hired me to watch out for you," Vrok told me.

A polite way of stating he was my bodyguard.

"We were just about to go into town to do a little shopping." Seyla kept peeking through her lashes at Vrok, who studiously ignored her.

"I'll be glad to accompany you," Vrok told me. He opened the front door of the shiny SUV. "Please. Have a seat, unless you'd prefer to drive."

"Drive your car?" I said.

"It's your vehicle, compliments of Tylik." He flashed me a sweet smile. "I can either drive or ride shotgun."

"I don't need a car."

"And yet, you now have one."

"Sometimes, it's just easier to go with the flow," Violet said, watching our interaction with amusement. From what I'd heard, she'd inherited the B&B from her grandmother, but there were conditions she had to fulfill to claim full title. Goreg stepped in and helped her fix the place up, as did his gargoyle brothers, and along the way, she and Goreg had fallen in love.

"But . . ." I sputtered, knowing she was right. When

Tylik and I got engaged, my focus had been on a baby and trying to keep from falling in love. But as his fiancée and later this week, his wife, I'd be expected to act like a sort-of elf/maybe duchess, and that would include riding in style.

"Thank you," I told Vrok. "You can drive."

"Huh," Seyla said, climbing into the backseat, frowning at Vrok.

CHAPTER 15
KATE

Vrok got into the driver's seat while I buckled. "Where would you like to go?" he asked.

Seyla leaned forward and named the store.

He gave her a curt nod. My friend was one of the sweetest people I know, and she could attract a guy even if she was covered in mud and wore a floor-length coat. She had the magnetic touch.

It would be interesting to see if Vrok could continue to ignore her or if he'd succumb like almost every other guy out there.

He started the SUV and backed down the drive, turning and taking the vehicle toward the downtown area.

His dragonette hopped off his shoulder and perched on the headrest, looking from me to Seyla. It extended its golden wings and stretched its neck out toward us.

"Behave, Merith," Vrok said. He reached toward the dragonette, but it took flight, soaring toward Seyla.

I sucked in a breath as it landed on her shoulder. It tilted its head, studying her face, before rubbing its cheek against hers.

She shot me a grin.

Vrok shot her a scowl before jerking his attention back to the road. "Come back here, Merith. I don't know what's gotten into him."

"He likes me," Seyla said, enchanted by the gorgeous creature.

Merith purred, still rubbing against her cheek.

"Can I touch him?" Seyla asked.

In the rearview mirror, I watched Vrok's lips thin, pressing against his tusks.

"I'd rather you didn't," he said. "Merith. On my shoulder."

"Maybe if you ask him nicely, he'll listen," Seyla said. "You're just a sweet little dragonette who needs love, aren't you?" she cooed at Merith.

When she stroked the tiny beast, his purrs grew louder.

He remained on her shoulder, soaking in her touch, until Vrok parked and got out of the car. When he opened my door, Merith left Seyla's shoulder and flew out the opening. He soared into the sky before swooping back down to land on Vrok's head.

Vrok heaved a sigh and lifted the dragonette, losing some hair to the creature's claws in the process, and placed Merith on his shoulder. He held Seyla's door open, and she grinned at him as she climbed out.

We entered the store. Inside, Vrok scanned the area

before standing near the door; his gaze locked on me. Merith watched us—watched Seyla, that is—just as intently.

"How about this one?" Seyla asked, holding out a pretty dark purple dress that would brush my ankles. "Love the bodice."

"I'll try it on." I collected a few more dresses, but before I could enter the changing room, Vrok snapped his arm between me and the open doorway. Merith squawked but remained on his shoulder.

"Allow me to ensure it's safe and secure." He poked his head inside before nodding. "All clear."

This could get tiresome. Or entertaining. It was all a matter of perspective.

"Can I be of assistance?" an older woman with long black hair highlighted with orange and yellow streaks asked. Seyla mentioned she was a phoenix. I'd heard a few had moved to town.

"I want to try these on," I said, lifting my arm draped with dresses.

"Of course." She smiled and took them from me, hanging them inside the changing room. "Let me know if I can bring you more. We've got plenty in your size."

That was a switch. It wasn't always easy finding cute stuff for a larger body without having to order online.

"Want my help?" Seyla asked as I started to shut the door. She shot Vrok a look of longing, something I'd never seen on her face before. She once told me she hated being the center of attention, that she wished more guys just wanted to be friends. She'd dated, but she hadn't been serious with many guys.

"Sure, come on in." I opened the door wider. "My maid of honor should be inside while I try on dresses." I watched her face.

Seyla clapped her hands to her cheeks. "Really? Me, your maid of honor?"

I barreled into her, giving her a hug. "Say yes, please."

"Yes, yes." She hopped around. "Imagine, a maid of honor. Me!"

I laughed. "Your first task is to help me pick out a few dresses."

"On it." She bustled me inside and made faces at her reflection in the mirror.

I tugged off my pants and shirt and shimmied into the first dress.

She did up the back and pivoted me to face the mirror. "Aw, Kate, you look gorgeous." A scrunch, and she'd swept up my hair. "Wear it like this. You're so pretty. I'm envious."

"What?" I gaped at her.

"Your hair, your curvy shape, and the way guys look at you like they want to eat you up."

I widened my eyes. "Are you talking about me?"

"Get this one," she said, undoing the dress. "On to the blue. And yes, I'm talking about you, silly. Have you seen how Tylik looks at you?"

"With gratitude?"

"Maybe at first, but I think he likes you. He sees you."

"That's a bit scary."

She dropped the blue dress over my head and fed my arms through the sleeves, then hugged me from behind. "Not scary at all when you're marrying him."

"You know why I am."

She shrugged. "Things can change. You can change."

"In what way?" I nibbled on my lower lip, staring into the mirror, but not really seeing my reflection. What we'd done yesterday . . . I kept thinking about his touch, his mouth on my breast . . .

My mind skipped along with my friend into a dream world where Tylik and I chose not to get divorced. Where we grew to love each other. Only danger and heartache lay in that direction.

"He looks at you in a good way. Ride with it, as Violet would say." She crinkled her face at me in the mirror. "Promise me you'll grab a wonderful opportunity if it's thrust beneath your nose."

"I don't know if I can make that promise."

"Blue looks good too. Now for the pink." She bustled me out of the dress and tugged the pink one over my head. "No way. Pepto explosion." Yanking it over my head, she helped me into a dark green sheath dress. "I know people say redheads shouldn't wear green, but just like your gown for the ball, this one looks amazing on you." She tapped my shoulder. "Please see the Kate I do, the one who's kind to everyone, who makes us laugh, and who deserves the best things in life."

When I squinted, I kinda saw the same Kate as my friend. Could I let myself bloom?

All I could do is try.

My mind may be changing about what I wanted regarding relationships, and I might want more with Tylik than I should, but he hadn't indicated he felt the same.

I wasn't falling in love with him, was I?

I suspected I was.

TYLIK

My fellow monsters could be quite accommodating. I placed a notice at my apothecary shop that I would be closing starting tomorrow through my honeymoon, and I not only heard understanding from my customers, but they also universally congratulated me on my upcoming nuptials.

Perhaps I was beginning to fit in, not only with monsters but also with humans?

After closing early, I collected Kate, and we took a flisteer carriage to my aunt's estate. Once we'd finished, I'd have my first driving lesson.

I couldn't wait.

"There you are," my aunt cried, striding across the foyer when we stepped inside. "Elisa and Raze arrived a short time ago to help us with the last parts of the menu. I've taken them to the front parlor and the staff is serving them beverages." Her gaze fell on Kate. "You look lovely, my dear. So lovely."

"Thank you," Kate said, blushing.

She did. It was all I could do to drag my eyes away from her.

We followed my aunt into the parlor.

Raze stood. "There you are." With a grin, he strode forward and braced my shoulders. "Nice to see you. Kate, you too." He dipped his head her way.

Elisa hugged Kate and then me, and my face heated. We were friends already, but something had changed. A few weeks ago, they never would've hugged me. They'd softened, perhaps because I was doing so myself? Whatever it was, I liked it.

"We'll get started when you're ready," my aunt said, waving to various seats. "Would you two like something to drink?"

Kate and I shook our heads.

"Storm told me today that everything's set for the main courses," Raze said, settling on a sofa beside Elisa and putting his arm around her shoulders.

"And Rylee's working on the cake," Elisa said. "She showed me some drawings. It's going to be gorgeous."

Hundreds of guests would attend our wedding, so Rylee would make an enormous cake, plus cupcakes, each decorated like the one she'd gifted us earlier in the week.

"What appetizers would you like?" Elisa asked Kate. She ran her fingers along Raze's thigh. They, like Gunner and Rylee, were so happy together it made my heart pinch tight. "We can arrange for anything."

"Mini weenies in blankets?" Kate chuckled. "I'm only kidding. They're kind of a backyard thing."

"I haven't heard of those before," Finni said with a bright smile. "I want to try them." She leaned forward to tap my knee. Kate and I sat together on another small sofa, and I was hyperaware of her at all times. It was all I could do to sleep last night. I kept thinking about what we'd done on my bed.

Soon, we'd share the bed. I was even more excited about that than learning to drive.

"What human foods have you tried so far?" my aunt asked me.

Ah, yes, she was quizzing me about my progress in learning about human customs.

"We're going for ice cream later," Kate said, jumping in smoothly.

Finni's head tilted. "One ices cream?"

"It's amazing," Raze said. "Sweet, cold, and it melts in your mouth. I keep it stocked at all times."

"I must try this," my aunt said. "Soon."

"Maybe we can bring you some," Kate said.

My aunt's eyes gleamed with excitement. "I will wait impatiently for it." She tapped her staff member's arm. "Write down wieners on your paper."

Elisa snorted, but she slapped her hand over her mouth, her eyes sparkling.

"*Weenies*," Raze smoothly corrected." A wiener is . . . Well, we won't be eating those in polite company."

Weiner . . . Realizing what he must mean, my own eyes widened, and I bit back a laugh.

My aunt caught on as well, and her laughter burst out. "Yes, we will not eat those at your wedding." With a shake of her head, she nodded at Kate. "What other human appetizers should we have? Tylik suggested a variety of elf dishes, but this is a mixing of our worlds, and your wedding meal should reflect that."

"How about . . ." Kate named a bunch of foods I'd heard of, though I hadn't tried more than a few. I tended to prepare my own meals inside my home, not "go out to eat" as so many others did.

"Delightful," Finni cried, tapping her fingertips as her staff member added each item to the list. She looked up at the stately elf. "Don't miss any of that."

We finished lining up the menu.

Finni looked between us. "What else do we need to speak about?"

"Decorations," Elisa said, consulting a list on her phone. "I was able to match the green you wanted, but I'm unsure about maroon. Would fuchsia work?"

"As long as it's not too pink," Kate said.

"Definitely not pink," Raze said. He and Elisa shared a glance I couldn't interpret. "Vrok's . . ."

That was right. Vrok and his fiancée had been working with Elisa and Raze to plan their wedding.

"His former fiancée loves pink," Elisa said. "Everything had to be that color."

"I like pink well enough," Kate said. "But you have to be careful when you combine it with green."

"I've ensured the ballroom will be completely decorated," my aunt said. "Under Raze and Elisa's direction of course."

"Thank you," I said.

"Seyla's taking me shopping for a gown tomorrow," Kate said. "The bridal shop said they'd have the dress ready by Saturday morning."

"Oh, that's much too close," my aunt said. "Select your gown and tell them to take your measurements and send them to me. My pixie friends will do it overnight. Their stitching is exquisite, and they'll be delighted to help with any alterations."

"Thank you." Kate squeezed my hand, and I loved how natural it felt to be close to her, feel her. "I can't believe pixies will work on my gown. I'm honored."

Finni dipped her head toward Kate, and when her gaze met mine, I noted respect. Kate had said just the right thing to please my aunt, though I knew Kate's words were spoken from her heart and not contrived to please anyone.

"Anything else?" Finni asked.

"I believe that's it." Elisa consulted her list once more. "You're handling so much of it here already. I feel like we're not doing more than supervising."

"You do it so well," Finni said. She beamed at me and Kate. "This is an important wedding, the joining of our people."

"If we're all set," I said, tugging Kate up to stand with me, "I have a driving lesson."

"We need to leave as well," Raze said. "I appreciate you taking the time to meet with us."

"Of course," my aunt said. "I'll recommend your services off the line."

Raze blinked a moment before his face cleared. "Online? That's very kind of you. Word of mouth is the best way to build a business."

"I'm sure many elves who choose to settle in this community will be reaching out," I said. "I'll happily share our experience with anyone who mentions they're planning a wedding."

"You're sweet," Elisa said, giving me a hug. They left while we lingered with my aunt.

"Will you return for dinner after your vehicle operation lesson?" my aunt asked as she walked with us to the front door. "I'm only having a few guests. It will feel cozy. We can visit some more." Her gaze took in Kate too.

Torn because I wanted to please my aunt, I looked Kate's way. She stared at me with a bemused expression, and I wasn't sure how to reply.

"Kate and I thought we'd have a quiet dinner together," I said.

"Ah, you two lovers wish to be alone." Aunt Finni grinned. "Far be it for me to separate you when you're so close to wedded bliss."

"Thank you." I bowed her way, then held out my hand to Kate. "Shall we?"

We left the castle and strode to one of the waiting flisteer carriages. I supposed we'd eventually send all the flisteers back to the fae realm and ride in internal combustion engine vehicles like humans.

"I don't remember plans for dinner," she said. "But the park sounds fun."

We settled inside the carriage and the creatures took off, soaring into the sky and over the tops of the trees.

The bemused expression hadn't left her face, but I wasn't sure how to interpret it. We knew each other much better now, but she was still an amazing mystery to me most of the time.

"Do you have someplace else you'd rather be?" I finally asked.

"That's a loaded question." Her chuckle rang out. "I should mention that Rylee gave me the rest of the week off and next week, too. She seemed to think we'll go on a honeymoon."

"We will." I'd been quizzing Vrok about human wedding customs, and he'd mentioned that one, sadly stating he and his former fiancée had cancelled their plans.

A honeymoon might be my only chance to convince Kate we were meant to be together. Once she was pregnant, I worried it would be over. My heart was going to be crushed when she announced it was time for us to divorce, but I hadn't yet figured out how to keep it from happening.

She shot me a smile. "I didn't think we'd go anywhere."

"No honeymoon?" I struggled to get the words out because they didn't share my true feelings. "My aunt will expect it." This had nothing to do with my aunt.

Her shoulders dropped. "Oh, yes, we need to make sure we keep up the ruse."

"Are you having second thoughts?"

"No." The word popped out. "Not one bit."

I took her hand. "I . . ." I shook my head. I couldn't share my growing feelings. I was falling in love with her, and there seemed to be no way to hold it back.

Could I convince her to feel the same? Love wasn't something you could control, as I'd quickly learned after meeting Kate. She liked me. We had fun together. She found pleasure in my touch.

We could build off that.

The flisteers continued pulling us toward town.

"Where are we going for our honeymoon?" she asked.

"Would it be bad of me to keep it a surprise?" I wanted everything to be perfect, and there was only one place I could think of that would fit.

"I like surprises," she said with a smile.

The flisteers soared toward the ground, landing lightly, the wheels rolling across the driveway to the B&B.

"You'll be amazed by this one."

CHAPTER 17

KATE

The flisteer carriage landed in the driveway, and we got out.

"I can't wait to operate this amazing machine," Tylik said, striding over to the SUV and patting it.

It was the most gorgeous car I'd ever owned, though I actually had never owned a vehicle. Me and Mom had always walked or taken public transportation.

Tylik continued to pat the vehicle. "Isn't your new internal combustion engine beautiful?"

I grinned because he was right. "It sure is. You don't need to call it an internal combustion engine, however. Most people would call it a car or an SUV."

"Ah, yes. To fit in, I'll consider putting aside the term I've used. At the vehicle seller, I told them you needed a bright one, that it should be the nicest beast they had to offer."

"I hope you didn't spend too much." Of course he

did. It was a new vehicle. "I hate that you've spent so much on me."

"You deserve this, though I suppose we could share it," he shook his head. "It's all yours, my lovely fiancée."

I savored him calling me lovely.

He was so cute and excited. There was no way I'd do anything to destroy that.

"I will say it's pretty," I said, handing him the fob.

He paused in the driveway. "Watch this. I trialed all the buttons before I selected it." He pressed the panic button, and the vehicle started flashing lights and beeping. "Amazing, isn't it?" he shouted over the uproar.

Dogs started barking, and the abominable snow couple walking on the walk hand-in-hand bolted, racing down the street and out of view.

The neighbors were going to kill me.

"Keep it down out there," someone said. We looked up to find Raze poking his head out the window of the second story of his barn apartment. He and Elisa rented it from Goreg and Violet. "Oh, jeez. It's that time, huh?" He grinned. "You two have fun!"

"You need to turn it off," I told Tylik.

"What?" Tylik asked. He was so entranced by the sounds and flashing lights that he was nearly hopping. He swayed his hips like it was a dance tune.

I pressed the button, silencing the car.

"It's loud," I said, my ears ringing.

"It sure is." He grinned at me before looking up at Raze. "Isn't it amazing?"

Raze chuckled. "I'll be curious to hear how this goes.

Stop in later if you have time" Chuckling, he backed out of the window and shut it.

"And look at this," Tylik said, pushing another button. The vehicle started, purring softly. "It engages with one touch."

Other than when Vrok took me and Seyla into town, I hadn't ridden in such a nice set of wheels, let alone driven one. And Tylik wanted to give this to me like it was a daisy he'd picked on the lawn. I still couldn't believe this was my life.

"And this." Another button made the back hatch slowly lift. "So simple. When you need to access the rear part of this carriage, you can do so from anywhere throughout the world."

"It won't work unless you're near the vehicle."

A frown formed on his face. "It's defective then. I'll obtain you a different vehicle."

"That's normal for all cars." I waved to the passenger seat. "Climb in and we'll go get your learner's permit."

"I spoke with Maxon, and he pulled some . . ." He tilted his head. "Maxon pulled some ropes. The D of the MV delivered this to me." He held up a card. "It says I'm permitted to operate an internal combustion engine powered carriage as long as I do so with a designated driver beside me. I mean vehicle or SUV." He flashed me a grin that made my knees weaken. "Regardless, the designated driver is you, Kate. Only you."

CHAPTER 18
TYLIK

"Slow down," Kate said, her tone more guttural than I liked. She hung onto something she called the sheet bar and braced her other hand on the dash. I wasn't sure why it was called a dash when it appeared to be made from a strange sort of plastic and didn't appear to be dashing anywhere. I'd learned about plastic while building my house; it was something I hadn't incorporated since it didn't come from nature.

"You can't go this fast on Main Street," she said.

I frowned at the speed-o-meter, noting forty. "You're right. I do apologize." I removed my foot from the pedal that seemed to want me to slam it all the way to the ground and allowed the carriage to slow.

No, not a *carriage*. A vehicle or car. I appreciated that Kate was teaching me the terms I needed to fit in with human society.

"We've driven enough, don't you think?" she said in a

thready voice. "We could turn around and return to the B&B."

"You're correct. I have had one hour of driving, which was recommended for each session in the manual I studied last evening." I took her hand, squeezing it, watching her face. "You're very sweet to help me with this. I can't wait until I can—"

Her other hand snapped out, jerking the wheel to the left before I drove the vehicle up onto the curb—for the second time.

"Turn it around," she said, shaking her head. She shot me a smile. "You're actually doing very well. It takes time to learn how to drive. We've got lots of time to teach you."

"Thank you."

"Of course."

"Tomorrow, I'll ask Vrok to take you into town when you select your wedding dress. He can drive you or you can operate the vehicle while he rides . . . shotgun." The term she'd used for where she sat. It made me laugh.

"I'm still not used to having a bodyguard, but it's nice letting someone else drive." She nudged her head, reminding me to pay attention to where I guided this vehicle. "If you'd like, we can stop at a coffee shop and get some drinks to have with our dinner at the park. Does iced coffee sound good?"

"I haven't had it. Many new experiences today. Driving. Iced coffee."

"You're going to love it all."

Under her direction, I took the vehicle into a parking lot and slowly drove around the back of the building, approaching the road again. Stopping completely at the sign, I looked both ways before cautiously pulling out among the other cars. When the DMV delivered my card that gave me permission to operate a vehicle such as this, they also gifted me a fascinating book full of many rules related to the operation of said vehicle. I'd studied it before taking a carriage to the B&B to collect Kate.

"The coffee place is up here." She pointed. "Put your blinker on and when you can safely turn, do so. Park in any spot—that would be between two lines in the lot."

I did as she requested, proud of how smoothly I handled this car. It would be a good vehicle for Kate to drive. She would be safe surrounded by this much metal.

"I obtained tea at this place once," I said, cringing as we stepped inside. "I'm afraid it was right after I'd arrived in the human realm, and I may have made some mistakes."

She linked her arm through mine. "No problem. I'll teach you all you need to know."

We joined the line, moving slowly toward the staff person I'd spoken with when I came here that one time.

When he saw me, he scowled. "You." His finger stabbed in my direction. "Get out of here."

"We're here for coffee," Kate said in a more pleasant tone than I felt was warranted.

"He's a shoplifter," the male growled. "Tried to walk out without paying the last time he was here. Seemed to think a coin he insisted was gold would be enough. Like I'd believe that? I didn't fall off the potato truck yesterday." His hand flapped our way. "Go. Don't come here again."

Silence descended in the big open room. Someone snickered behind us.

"Let me tell you, buddy," Kate snarled, glaring at the male. "First, he's an elf, and he's new to our world, which means he deserves our respect and patience."

The guy sputtered, frowning. "Well, I—"

"*Second*, he just wanted tea," she half-shouted.

"He got his—"

"*Third*, his coin *was* gold, so you messed that one up." With a huff, she pivoted, still holding my arm and taking me with her. Her voice lifted even higher, and she spoke to the room in general. "You'll get much better food at Rylee's bakery, *Love at First Bite*. Her muffins melt in your mouth, and her coffee comes from freshly ground beans she imports from Costa Rica. It's much better than anything they serve *here*."

She took me outside, where she stormed back and forth in front of her vehicle. "The nerve of him."

"You're amazing."

"What?"

I grinned. "You taught me so much already. Now I owe you something in exchange."

She frowned up at me as I tugged her closer.

I captured her mouth and laid her back on the hood of our car.

With a moan, she latched onto my shoulders.

And because I could and I suspected it would irritate the owner of this shop, I pressed the panic button, making the car honk shrilly.

CHAPTER 19
TYLIK

"We forgot to arrange for our dinner," Kate said as we pulled into the park.

"Monstrous Munchies is delivering." I'd placed an order this morning, walking into the shop—by myself and without Kate giving direction.

I couldn't quite believe how far I'd come. Me, ordering food like those around me. Although, I hadn't felt much like a human activity since the owner was an orc.

"Annalisa's food is so good," Kate said.

We got out of my car and, holding hands, meandered along a path weaving through the park, arriving at tables beneath a cluster of trees.

The heat of the day had fled, leaving balmy air behind. We weren't the only ones taking advantage of the nice weather.

A yeti couple and their eight young of varying ages had taken over the table next to ours. And a centaur family played with a flying disk in the open area nearby.

The yeti dad grinned my way and nodded approval of Kate.

She was perfect. I knew that already. Pride made my chest puff, and I nodded to him about his mate.

His chest inflated like mine, and we both laughed.

"What?" Kate asked, smiling.

"Nothing." Leaning across the table, I kissed her, loving how she responded to my touch.

By the time I retook my seat, the yeti dad had gone back to bouncing his new babe on his knee. Catching my eye, his child grinned. He squealed with joy, and there couldn't be anything better than that.

"You're very good with children," Kate said, watching the interaction. Her smile fell fast, and I knew why. She was thinking of us having a baby and then separating.

It was too easy to see myself cuddling our child during the day and holding Kate close all night.

I was definitely going to get hurt, but I couldn't seem to stop it from happening.

I didn't want our time together to be tainted with sorrow, however. "I expect our food to arrive in—"

"There you are," Annalisa exclaimed, striding up the path and stopping beside our table. She placed the bag containing our food between us. "Just the way you requested, Tylik." She nodded Kate's way. "How are you?"

"Great, thanks. The weather's gorgeous, isn't it?"

"It sure is. I love this time of year the most," Annalisa

said. "I heard through a secret source that you two are engaged." She winked at Kate. "Quite a catch you've made there."

"Tylik's amazing." She smiled my way, and I wished the excitement I saw in her eyes was because she was eager to be with me always.

"He sure is," Annalisa said.

"I'm the one who's lucky," I pointed out. "Kate's amazing too."

"You're so sweet. In fact—" Annalisa frowned, and her head tilted. "Ah, just on time."

A swooping sound rang out overhead, and we all looked up, even the yeti children, who went silent.

The gargoyle, Murtik, flew in and landed on the grass a short distance away, his gaze locked on Annalisa. His wings folded against his spine as he strode forward with enough bluster to make me wince.

Annalisa's smile never wavered, though she did roll her eyes at Kate, who chuckled.

"There you are," Murtik said, joining us, though his gaze was only for Annalisa. "I thought I might find you here."

"What gave you that idea?"

He frowned, and his head tilted as if he couldn't figure her out. "I work for you now, remember?"

"You do?" I asked.

"Tylik," he said, bowing toward me. "Kate." He took her hand and kissed it.

She shot me an eyebrow-raised look.

Annalisa's smile dropped faster than a rock rolling

down a hillside.

"Enjoy your meal," she said to us without inflection. She pivoted and strode back toward the parking lot.

"Wait," Murtik cried, half running, half flying/hopping after her.

She stopped on the path and turned to face him, her hands smacking on her hips. "I told you to remain at the shop."

"I thought I could give you a ride back."

Her hand jutted out, and her green orc face darkened. "And what am I supposed to do with my vehicle, leave it here?"

"I'm sorry." His wings drooped. "You're right. I've made a mistake."

"I can't figure out why I hired you." Her grumble rang out.

"Because I make a great sandwich." His wings fluttered gargoyle flirtation before settling back into the usual position.

"Not exactly," she said. "I wanted a chance to get to know you better."

"Of course you did," Murtik said with a grin.

"And you know what I've discovered since then?"

He shook his head.

I cringed, waiting.

"I've discovered that while there's definitely attraction between us, I don't believe I *want* to like you, Murtik. You flirt with every female who comes into the shop."

He stiffened. "I'm polite."

Her hand lifted Kate's way. "You kiss whoever you

can."

"Not on the lips."

"Don't you see what I'm saying?"

He shook his head, and from where I was sitting, he appeared stunned. She may be the first person to tell him what he needed to hear.

"We spent a night together, Murtik." Her voice broke, and her shoulders curled forward.

"It was wonderful." He reached out to her. "I've never felt this way about anyone before."

Her chin lifted, and her eyes shimmered with tears. "You have a poor way of showing it." Her heavy sigh rang out. "I see a guy who says he wants to be with me but who acts like he's equally happy to be with every single female in this town if they'll let him." Her voice shook. "I thought we had something special, Murtik. I thought if we worked together, we'd grow closer, that you'd come to care for me, but I don't think I can keep trying any longer." Turning, she walked toward the parking lot.

He stared after her, still stunned, before his low voice rang out. "Annalisa, wait. Wait!"

He took flight, soaring over her as she got into her car and started it up. When she drove it out onto the road, he flew overhead, watching and protecting her.

"Well," Kate said, "I'm not sure who I'm rooting for in that relationship."

"I believe Murtik has met his match, as they say," I said. "I also bet he didn't realize that fact until now. I hope he sees he's going to have to grovel, or he'll lose the best thing in his life."

CHAPTER 20

KATE

I barely slept that night. All I could think of was the fact that I was moving in with Tylik in the afternoon.

And then I dreamed of trying on a thousand wedding dresses. Only one fit and it was covered with so much lace the parts on the bodice kept flipping up to hit me in the cheeks.

Thankfully, by morning I dreamed I'd found the right one, and it looked fantastic.

Despite deciding I wouldn't marry after Dad left Mom, that didn't mean the idea hadn't flitted through my mind every now and then. Didn't most people picture what they'd wear and what kind of ceremony they'd like to have?

As I showered, I came to a decision. Days ago, I'd assumed I'd pick something random. I wanted to look good, but who needed a dream gown for a wedding that would end once I was pregnant?

Now that I was falling in love with Tylik, I wanted

that dream gown, one I'd proudly wear when I walked down the aisle.

A car turned into the driveway at 10:45 a.m.

"He's here," Seyla whispered, staring out my window at the driveway below.

"Who?" I joined her, watching as Vrok got out of his own vehicle and came up the path to the entrance of the B&B.

"He's so nice," she said wistfully. "I wish he liked me as much as his cute little dragonette does. Now *he's* a dragon I'd love to make purr."

I chuckled. "He's an orc, not a dragon."

Her head tilted. "Do you think dragons are real?"

"Dragonettes are."

"Huh."

"Talk to him today," I said, tugging on my jeans. I went to my bureau for socks. "I'll be busy trying on dresses, and he'll be doing bodyguard things."

"No way." She turned from the window. "You're trying on dresses. I want to be inside the changing room with you helping zip or button up each one. In between then, I'll be scouring the shop for other dresses. Romance —or the lack of it in Vrok's case—can wait. Friends are forever."

And this was another reason why I was never jealous of Seyla. She was one of those truly nice people who spoke what was in her heart.

"I thought I'd be the one watching you try on dresses, never me," I said.

"Someday maybe," she said wistfully. "I haven't

given up yet. Enough about me, though. How are things going with you and Tylik?" She took my hand and tugged me over to sit on the bed beside her—another sign of pure friendship. A guy she liked was waiting on the front porch for us to come down, but she wanted to give me the chance to speak my thoughts instead of scooting downstairs to stare at him.

"Things are going well." I injected a bunch of cheer into my voice.

"You're not telling me something." Her sharp eyes missed nothing.

"I'm falling for him, and I can't seem to stop it from happening." I turned to face her, tucking my heel under my butt.

"So he's more than a baby daddy."

"I wish." I sighed. "I mean, he'll make a great father, and I know he'll respect whatever rules I lay down about parental rights, but what if . . .?"

"What if you want more?" She rubbed my arms. "It's okay to fall in love. He's a wonderful guy."

"I'm moving in with him later today. Tonight . . ."

"You said he told you he'll wait until you're ready."

"Oh, I'm ready," I said. More than ready. I craved him like no one else before. "What if he isn't?"

"I'm sure he's ready too," she quipped, her smile quickly smoothing, though her eyes continued to sparkle. "Are you sure he doesn't want you just as much, and I don't mean for sex?"

"I haven't asked him. How can I?"

"After what happened the other day?"

I'd shared some of what went on inside his bedroom, skimming over it. She knew we'd done a few things, but I didn't tell her everything.

"Do you think it was a heat of the moment thing for him?" I asked. No, I *pleaded*. I needed her to tell me it was going to work out, that he'd fall for me, and when we had a baby, we'd raise it together.

"Tylik's a hot elf. He's pretty much aristocracy. He can have any woman he wants."

My lips twisted. "This isn't making me feel better."

She gave me a soft smile. "He chose *you*."

"I proposed to him."

"He could've turned you down. Look at how I see it. He was at a ball. Women were throwing themselves at him."

"Definitely not helping!"

"You know what I mean. If he didn't want to be with you—*you*, not any of the other women there that night—he would've politely turned you down."

"I gave him an easy solution to his problem."

"And now you regret it?"

"No, I can't," I said. "If I hadn't proposed, would he have seen me?"

"You forget what a nice person you are, how your goodness shines through. Everyone sees it but you."

"I can't see myself."

"Then look in a mirror." Rising, she dragged me off the bed and over to the oval mirror hanging on the wall, turning me to face it. "Take a good look."

"I've seen myself a billion times." I didn't have time

for this. We had to get to the store. I had an appointment. I still had more packing to do, though most of my things were still in boxes after moving here.

She reached up and held my chin still. "I don't think you've ever seen yourself like I do."

I pinched my eyes shut before opening them to look in the mirror. Same red hair—my best feature. Blue eyes. Pointy chin with a tiny dimple. Not too much double chin, though I didn't lower my jaw or turn sideways to test it. Nice eyebrows, but I'd plucked them—

"You're only seeing your physical appearance," Seyla said. "Stare into your eyes and look past the color."

I didn't like doing that because . . . "I see loneliness."

"I see a sweet person who just needs to find the right guy to love. I think that's Tylik."

"What if he leaves me like my dad did?"

"You mean emotionally abandons you like your mom."

"Yeah, she did that." I knew this; my friend was only naming it, bringing it out into the full light. "What if I get pregnant and he says, oh, hey, it's time for that divorce? Here are the papers; sign here."

"If he doesn't see who you really are by then, good riddance."

"I'll be hurt."

"Won't you be hurt if you don't try?"

That made me pause. Tears sprung up in my eyes. "You're making me examine my heart too closely. I don't like it."

She shrugged. "Then you'll always be lonely, and

that's a true tragedy, because the Kate I know deserves the best in life. That's Tylik. You just have to meet him halfway."

"I'm afraid."

"Your family did a number on you. Are you sure you want to let them continue to control your thoughts and actions?"

"They aren't."

"If they weren't, you wouldn't be afraid. You'd shed them like a snake with an old skin and slither away from them straight into Tylik's arms."

Turning to face her, I gave her a watery smile. "I hate how you make me think all the time."

"And that's why we're best friends."

CHAPTER 21
TYLIK

I was playing with fire, and its name was Kate. But she was moving in with me today.

Naturally, I'd barely slept last night.

Rising early, I'd washed my bedding and cleaned my home from the top to the bottom. It was only when I was weeding the flower beds that I realized what I was doing. I wanted everything to be perfect so she'd have no reason to reject me.

Because I loved her. I'd slipped into the emotion easily, yet it felt right. She was the one I would adore for the rest of my days. If only she could feel the same.

Soon, we'd put our relationship to the final test.

After cleaning, I paced in my home. I'd offered to help Kate bring her things over, but she'd insisted she'd already packed the SUV and would drive over herself. Vrok would follow her in his own vehicle to ensure she arrived safely.

Before the wedding, I planned to extract my aunt's

promise to make my sister a duchess, relieving me of a cursed dukedom.

Everything was coming together. In two days, we'd marry and begin our new life together.

The only thing left was for Kate to fall in love with me.

Tonight, we'd lie in the same bed. My body throbbed for her. My soul craved her like no other. My heart had been rent asunder and only Kate's love could fuse it back together.

"I won't push her for anything she doesn't want to do," I said softly. "I'll sleep in the loft tonight. She can have the bed."

I paced some more, my footsteps dull thuds on the floor.

Crossing to the fireplace, I stared at the logs in the grate. Should I light a fire? It was hot outside, but I'd read on the line—no, *online*—that humans enjoyed fire, that they found a sense of security in the flames. Some still used it for heat, but the majority lit fires for aesthetic reasons. Hence the pit the builders suggested I place in my backyard. I had yet to use it because I wasn't sure why anyone would wish to light a fire and sit beside it.

Especially since I was alone.

But Kate would be here tonight. She might enjoy sitting by the flames. It could protect her, warm her, and give her joy—all things I wanted to do myself.

"Maybe she doesn't enjoy fire," I said to the fireplace.

"I do."

I turned to find her right behind me. Startled, I stepped backward.

Her smile fell. "Sorry. I knocked, but I guess you didn't hear me. You said to come in when I got here, not to stand outside, but . . . This is your home."

I took her hands and tugged her into my arms. "This is your home too." Now, it would be ours for as long as she remained with me.

"Alright." She lifted a smile, but it trembled. Was she as nervous about this as me? A week ago, we hadn't known the other existed. I couldn't imagine not knowing her, not sharing my life with her.

I was going to be so lonely once she left me.

No, I couldn't look at it that way. I knew from the start this was a temporary arrangement. It wasn't her fault I wanted to change the rules.

"Let me help you bring in your things," I said.

It didn't take long to carry in her boxes, and my heart hurt to see how few possessions she had.

"I travel light," she said, her hands twitching. "When Seyla and I moved here, we had to ship our things. It was super expensive, so I was careful to send only what I felt I couldn't live without."

"We can retrieve your other possessions."

"I gave most of them to a thrift store or friends." Her gaze swept across the four boxes and a case on wheels that must hold her clothing. "Other than the bags holding my new dresses lying across the SUV's backseat, this is it."

"I'll buy you new things, then."

"I'm going to say yes." A true grin rose on her face, and my heartache eased. "You know me, always saying no, don't buy me this or don't buy me that, but I've been talking firmly to myself."

"What has your inner Kate been saying?" I loved seeing this happy Kate. When she was sad, so was I. Now I wanted to smile and laugh because I'd do it with her.

"She told me I was going to be your wife. That this would be my home and you'd be my husband. That it was okay to accept things from you. That it didn't mean I was taking it from someone else. Not all the time, that is."

"Why would me giving you things take them from others?"

"My mom's exceedingly generous. She would give the shirt off her back to someone in need, as they say. It's true, though; I've seen her do it. I was raised with that thought in mind."

"Doing without yourself so others might have their needs filled."

"Exactly."

"But what about Kate? She must have needs, ones that shouldn't be given away."

She looked up at me, so earnest. "I do have needs."

"What do you want, Kate?" I said softly.

"You, Tylik. I want you."

I wasn't baring my soul or telling him everything in my heart, though I sensed that day would arrive soon. Love was meant to be shared just like money and possessions, my mom always said. She was right. Holding my feelings inside made them tangle together. I wanted to slip them free and hand them to Tylik no matter what might come from my confession.

Tomorrow, after our wedding and when we were taking the first step of our new lives, I was going to tell him I loved him.

He could reject me, or he might open his arms.

I wasn't pinning my feelings inside any longer. Sharing might result in pain, but it hurt just as much when I held it inside.

"Kate," he groaned, tugging me closer. "Do you mean you want me to . . . help you unpack or go with you for the ice cream we forgot to get last night or make sure the flowers are not wilting?"

"No," I gulped. "I want to take our clothing off and go to your bedroom."

His pupils dilated. "We won't be sleeping if we do something like that."

My laugh burst out. "I have a feeling we might not get much sleep tonight as it is."

"Do you mean this, Kate?" Sweet vulnerability came through in his voice. I couldn't believe this big, burly guy cared about what I had to say.

"I do." If he hadn't given me some sort of sign, I was going to chicken out and suggest we go get ice cream. But as much as I loved cookies and cream, I wanted him more. I poked his chest. "Take that shirt off."

One side of his mouth quirked up. "I will if you do the same."

"One shirt off." I grabbed the hem and ripped it up over my head, tossing it on the floor.

His gaze was fixed on my boobs. "That garment you wear too."

"Bra."

"Yes, that bra must be removed."

"You're overdressed, Tylik."

He ripped his tunic off and chucked it. "I want to buy shirts such as yours. Also those that have fastenings up the front and sleeves coming to my wrists. The ones with patterns in straight lines. The fuzzy ones."

Fuzzy . . . "Oh, you mean flannel shirts?"

"Yes. Vrok wears them as does Raze, though not long ago, Raze always wore dark suits with white shirts and neck chokers."

"Yes, he did." I'd explain ties later. "We'll go shopping on our honeymoon."

"We will."

It was all I could do to think. His chest was amazing, a mass of rippling muscles and a light sprinkling of hair that etched down the middle of his abs, stopping at the top of his pants. I wanted to follow that trail more than anything.

Reaching back, I undid my bra, throwing it toward my shirt.

He gaped. "You . . . You are so lovely, Kate." He reached toward me, but I took a step backward.

"Pants," I said, feeling greedy. If I started touching him and he did the same with me, I was going to lose my mind. All I'd be able to do was feel. I wanted skin on skin when that happened.

"We could remove them at the same time," he said.

"Do you wear undies?"

"Undies?"

"Underwear, undergarments. Some women wear panties. Guys often wear boxers, briefs, and a few go commando."

His fingers froze at the top of his pants. "What would you have me command?"

"Whatever you wish to do." I pulled down my pants and straightened, flicking the pretty pink panties I'd put on not long ago. Plans had built inside me as I drove here, and they didn't include me showing off grannie panties.

His smoldering eyes traveled down my frame. "You will remove those," he growled.

"You're behind, Tylik. Ditch the pants, and I'll ditch my panties, and then I'm going to climb all over you."

He ripped off his pants, actually shredding them. No undies, but I was okay with that.

My panties joined the rest of my clothing on the floor.

When he held out his arms, I leapt into them.

CHAPTER 23
TYLIK

I was holding the woman I loved in my arms, and she wanted me. Me. Not some random male to give her a baby, but me.

There wasn't anything I wanted to do more than love her.

Pivoting on my heel, I carried her into my bedroom and laid her on the bed, climbing over her, straddling her hips with my thighs.

I leaned forward and kissed her.

She burst into bloom in my arms like the most delicate flower, heady and lovely beyond belief.

Her arms wrapped around my shoulders, and a moan worked through her, the hum of it vibrating across my skin.

Her hips lifted, bumping against me, and it was all I could do to focus on each second. I wanted to let my passion consume me, but I worried I'd scorch her alive with the emotion boiling within my heart.

Easing to her side, I continued kissing her while her hands stroked my arms and back. I slid my fingers down her side, using the most delicate touch. She shivered and released another moan. At her hips, I gripped tight before moving my hand between her legs, parting her thighs.

When I ran my thumb down her crease, I groaned. Damn, she was wet. Did she crave me as much as I did her?

I slid a finger inside her and groaned some more.

While she pumped up to meet me, I entwined my fingers inside her, moving them fast. I kissed her jaw and down to her breasts, where I sucked one of her nipples into my mouth. I rolled it, running my tongue across it.

"Tylik," she cried, arching her spine to push her breast closer.

I ran my thumb across her clit, savoring her heightened cries when I did it.

"I'm going to come too fast," she hissed. "Please. I need you."

Who was I to ignore her plea? I'd give her everything. My heart was hers already. My life she could claim forever if she wished. And now my body.

I rose over her and as I centered my cock at her opening, she hitched her legs around me, tugging at me to bring me closer.

With my eyes locked on hers, I thrust forward, pushing myself inside her.

We both moaned.

Her head thrashed on the bed as I started moving,

slowly at first, then faster at her urging. Her body sucked on my cock in a greedy way that made my pulse roar through me. I wasn't going to be able to hold back for long, though I would. I needed to feel her falling apart around me.

"Yes," she cried, clinging to my arms as I moved within her.

I'd never been with anyone I loved more, which meant this needed to be as wonderful for her as it was for me.

I lifted her hips and moved faster, pounding into her as she cried out yes and please and take me, Tylik. What could be better than loving the woman I'd adore for the rest of my days?

When she started to shudder, to give into her bliss, I wanted to make it better. Reaching between us, I found her clit, and I rode it as I rode her, crashing into her like a storm pummeling the shore.

She shattered with a heavy groan, clinging to me while her body gave into her bliss.

I drove it onward, tugging her up another cliff then riding down the other side with her.

When she collapsed beneath me a second time, I finally gave in, shooting myself inside her.

CHAPTER 24
KATE

"We need to eat ice cream for breakfast," I said the next morning. I felt giddy. Fulfilled. Sublimely happy. "And since we have the day off, let's do something fun."

"What do you have in mind?" he asked, crawling over me.

What was ice cream? I couldn't remember.

We started kissing, and soon, I was moaning while his palms glided down my side.

He parted my thighs and kissed down my body. When he sucked my clit into his mouth, my breath caught. Damn, he had an amazing tongue. It was thick and long, and when he drove it inside me, I nearly came on the spot.

He teased me with light licks, then deepened them until I was frantic, clinging to his long, silky hair. His tongue danced up and down my slit, flicking over my clit, keeping me craving more. He had a way of reading me;

he knew exactly how to touch me, how to caress me to drive me wilder than I could ever imagine.

The sensation of his wet mouth intensified the emotions coursing through my body.

My breathing quickened, my mind alighting with sensations unlike any I'd felt before.

His hot breath on my skin sent tiny electric shocks through me, and I bucked in response. I quivered with anticipation as he continued to explore me, plunging his tongue inside me until I was so aroused, I couldn't think of anything but him.

His hands came into play, cupping and squeezing my curves before sliding up to my breasts, bringing my nipples to hard peeks.

When he gently nibbled on my clit, I let go, calling out his name as spirals of light flickered behind my closed eyelids.

He turned me over on the bed and lifted my hips. A jerk of his body forward, and he drove himself deep inside me.

Our groans rang out.

He began to move, each thrust sending heat through my veins. In no time, I was with him again, soaring ever higher.

When I began to quiver, he reached beneath me and rolled my clit.

It didn't take more than that for me to explode.

I rode the waves as he plunged inside me. When he came with a heady groan, we collapsed on the bed, joined together once more.

CHAPTER 25
TYLIK

I drove the SUV to the ice cream place, stopping at crosswalks for anyone even contemplating leaving the sidewalk.

"You're doing very well," Kate said. "I bet you'll pass your test the first time around."

"Test?"

She glanced my way. "You have to pass a test with a driver from the state. If you do, you're granted a license. There are some limitations about who you can ride with for the first few months, but after that, you're the same as any other driver on the road. We should get you a cell phone one of these days too."

"Why would I need one of those?"

"You may want to call someone."

"I can visit them if I wish to speak with them."

"But what if it's raining or snowing?" she asked. "Wouldn't it be easier to pick up your cell phone and call, say, Raze, to talk without having to walk, take a carriage, or drive to him first?"

"I suppose. It's a human thing, and I do need to fit in."

She took my hand, squeezing it. "Don't do anything that doesn't feel right for you."

"This is my aunt's wish."

"What about Tylik's wish? That matters more to me." She pointed. "Pull in there on the right, Frank's Dairy Bar."

"Ice cream is a dairy product?"

"It is."

I couldn't imagine why people were thrilled with dairy products enough that they'd build a shop to cater solely to them, but perhaps my mind would be changed.

I carefully parked the SUV in a spot, ensuring the vehicle was as close as possible to the center to avoid doors banging together or creating too narrow a space for other vehicles.

We got out and walked up to the counter hand-in-hand to place our order. I couldn't stop smiling. I'd been grinning so long, my cheeks ached. What we'd shared last night and this morning made my life complete. I'd marry Kate tomorrow, and while we hadn't spoken about where our relationship would go after that, I suspected divorce might no longer loom on the horizon.

I loved her, and I would tell her tomorrow night after we'd wed.

"I can't believe you and your aunt haven't had ice

cream," Kate said, leaning into my side and looking up at me as I perused the endless flavor choices.

"I'm sure I'll berate myself later for avoiding this treat." Frowning, I held in my cringe. "One makes a dairy product treat from moose?"

"Moose . . ." Her eyes widened. "Oh, Moose Tracks. No moose meat in that. It's vanilla with fudge sauce and tiny peanut butter cups."

"Ah. I can't imagine such a thing. What is pee-noot butter? Butter, I am familiar with. We have something similar to that in the fae realm. I'm not sure about pee in my iced cream, however."

"Butter is wonderful. Hot bread slathered with it? I die on the spot. As for *peanut* butter, a peanut is a nut. Or a legume." Her head tilted. "I'm not sure which, but it's amazing. I bet you'll like it."

"I cannot picture legumes in dairy treats either."

"Why don't we get bowls with a few scoops of each? Then you can try a bunch of them." She waved to tables where families and couples sat, eating.

"Alright. You choose them, and I promise to try each."

"Cool," she breathed, frowning at the list. "Moose Tracks, of course, plus cookies and cream, coffee, since we missed out on the iced variety the other day. Hmm . . . How about strawberry, chocolate, and butter pecan?"

"Many nuts," I said, unsure why anyone would enjoy hard crunchy things in what appeared to be a smooth product, if those passing us with round blobs on brown tapered sticks were anything to go by.

"Those are cones," she said, nudging her head to someone passing us, holding two. "We'll try it that way another time. Cones not only hold the ice cream while you eat it, but you can also eat the cone after."

"You eat the container?"

"I guess you could say that," she said with a laugh. "They're crunchy and sweet like a cookie."

I'd reserve judgement. To me, they looked like the cardboard Kate used to pack her belongings.

Kate placed our order and started to pay.

"I have gold coins," I pointed out, offering one.

The young male behind the glass watched us, and his eager eyes locked on the coin. "I'm more than happy to take gold if you'd like," he said. "You're an elf, right? The ears and hair give you away."

"I am," I said with a dip of my head.

"One or two gold coins will be plenty," he said with an easy grin.

"Nope." Kate scowled at the male, which made no sense to me. He was making this simple for us. "Run the debit card, please."

The male huffed. "If you say so." He gazed longingly at me.

Kate lifted the tray loaded with two dishes, each holding a round blob of creamy confection and plastic spoons. Paper products to wipe our mouths after we ate completed our order.

As she started toward a table, I tossed the young male a gold coin.

"For your troubles," I said softly.

"Oh, cool," he breathed. "Come back soon!"

With a grin, I followed Kate, sitting beside her at a table. I nodded to a phoenix sitting on the other end, alone. He slowly ate a cone with a white cream topping. Like other phoenixes, he was tall and had a bulky build, plus lightly feathered wings lying tightly against his back. His dark hair and wings were shot through with orange and gold, the gold matching his eyes and his skin tone.

Kate handed me the scrap of paper, placing her own on her lap. I did the same.

"Dig in," she said, watching me.

"Aren't you going to eat too?"

"I have to watch the amazement appear on your face first. Go ahead." She prodded one of the white blobs with the tip of her spoon. This one had brown lumps in it, which couldn't be tasty. "That's Moose Tracks."

In case it tasted horrible, I scooped only a tiny bit into my spoon.

I held it up, scrutinizing it for a long while.

The swirling colors—deep brown and a creamy white—were inviting. It smelled sweet, a good thing. If I hated it, it would disappoint Kate. And while she was correct that I must use my own needs and wishes to guide me in my exploration of and assimilation into this world, I wanted to please her.

I loved her and seeing the joy on her face when I experienced new things made the less desirable activities and cultural aspects of this realm more appealing.

As soon as I placed the spoonful into my mouth, I

knew I'd found something nearly as wonderful as licking Kate. The texture was smooth, yet indulgent to the tongue. It was divine—not too sweet, not too rich, but a perfect balance between the two. The crunchy lump I'd expected to taste nasty gave me a delightful surprise. It melted on my tongue much too fast.

"We need to get large cones for my aunt," I declared while Kate grinned.

"Like it, huh?"

"Almost as tasty as you," I said in her ear.

"Then try this one next." She scooped up a pink blob and held it out to me.

This one was nearly as good as the Moose Tracks. By the time I'd finished trying them all, I'd found my favorite—coffee.

"Oh, shit," the phoenix sitting at our table cried out. He stood abruptly, and his ice cream dropped from his hand, landing with a smack on the wooden table.

His wings flared out, the gold catching the sunlight. He peered around. "Where is she?"

With a gasp, he burst into flames.

A few humans cried out.

We monsters watched.

"What . . .? What . . .?" Kate said, rising to rush toward him.

I held her back. "It's okay."

Within seconds, he stopped burning and with a poof, he disappeared, leaving only a charred puff of smoke coiling toward the ground and a few feathers until . . . A pop, and he reformed as a big bird in colors that rivaled a glorious sunset.

"And . . ." I said, holding up my hand. I dropped it on the table, and in a blink, the bird transformed back into the phoenix who'd been eating when we arrived.

Kate shot me a wide-eyed look. "Wow," she said softly. Her eyes widened even further. "He's . . ."

"Yup, naked." Rising, I tugged off my shirt to hand to him, but he held up his hand. One of them that is. The other cupped his package.

The phoenix tugged boxers out of a bag he'd left on the table. He sat and wrangled into them before standing. He stared down at his melting ice cream sadly before he left, striding across the parking lot with his bag slung over his bare back.

"I've never seen anything like that before," Kate said. "Does it hurt?"

"I don't believe so."

"A bit sad," she said.

"Losing his ice cream or reappearing completely naked?"

"Both. I mean, he looked upset. I'm sure he's embarrassed by it."

I shrugged. "I don't know much about phoenixes, but I imagine I'd be."

We dropped our empty dishes in a barrel and started toward the counter to purchase containers for my aunt.

"We'll zip over there and put them in the freezer," Kate said. "I can't wait to hear what she thinks."

Since a line had formed again, I opted to kiss my

fiancée. It was only when the young male server laughed that we broke apart, finding the line gone.

"We would like to order more," I told him.

"You can have whatever you'd like," he said.

Such a nice young male. He even added a large clump of paper face wipes to our order.

That was why I gave him *two* gold coins after taking the containers.

CHAPTER 26
KATE

Tylik insisted on going shopping after getting ice cream, so after we dropped the containers off at the estate, we headed back into town where he bought me enough clothing to triple my wardrobe.

After putting everything away, we had a snack and sat in his backyard, savoring the warm afternoon and just being together.

Then we went inside to get ready for dinner. And if it took us a bit longer than we'd expected to dress, that was okay. He'd been tasting me a lot lately, and it was time he had a turn.

As the sun started sliding toward the horizon, he drove us to the estate, parking out front.

Finni strode out the door held open by an elf, stopping on the big granite top step.

"You are operating an internal combustion engine," she exclaimed, tapping her fingertips together.

"I have my learner's permit," Tylik said as he put his

arm around me. We took the steps to the top. "I'm driving, and if your staff didn't mention it, we collected ice cream for you and placed it in your cold storage. You must try Moose Tracks. Coffee's my favorite, so we included that as well."

"I can't wait to try it." She studied Tylik with heavy intensity. "I see changes in you, nephew, and I like them." Her beaming gaze slid to me. "I believe I know why."

Heat rose into my face. For a fake relationship, we'd done much better than could be expected. I couldn't wait to get married to Tylik and . . . Did I dare hope this was a new and lasting beginning for us both?

I'd find out tomorrow.

"Have you made your decision yet?" Tylik asked his aunt.

"Let's see how things go at the wedding tomorrow, shall we?" she said. "If your human wedding goes without incident, I believe I'll be convinced."

Then we could only hope we had no issues. How could we? We'd thought of everything.

"Come inside," she said, turning.

We followed her into the foyer, but instead of going straight to the front parlor, her favorite spot, she paused by the stairs.

"The jewel room is ready," she said. "It's time we rectified your lack of a ring." Her pointed gaze fell on my hand, but I sensed her message was for Tylik. "I'll see you at the top?"

At Tylik's nod, she rounded the staircase to take the

lift installed behind it. Since it was small, we'd use the stairs.

I linked my arm through his, and we climbed the enormous staircase that spiraled all the way to the top of the multi-story structure.

"Just want to say that this place makes me nervous," I whispered. "It's so . . . grand. And big. And . . ."

"Too opulent, right? I completely agree," he said softly.

"I'm glad we live in your hobbit house."

"*Our* hobbit house," he said with a grin that made me love him even more.

We left the stairs and proceeded along a wide balcony overlooking the great hall below with rooms on our left. At the end, an elf guard bowed and swept open the door to a room spanning the front of the castle. It overlooked the lawn, the enormous fountain shaped like a dragon coiling toward the sky, plus the long, sweeping driveway. Far below and on a clear day, I bet you could see the entire town, as if Finni oversaw everything going on in front of her.

"There you are," she said, waiting inside the room. Her attention fell on me, and the skin around her eyes crinkled. "I neglected to mention, Kate. You look lovely, my dear. Simply lovely."

"Thank you," I said, grateful she was so kind.

"Shall we pick out your engagement ring?" she asked.

Without waiting for a reply, she took my arm and led me through the room with an inner wall made up completely of dark glass. In the center, she waved her hand, and a click rang out.

"I do love the tiny bits of magic we were allowed to bring with us," she said, shooting me a smile.

"You use magic for security?" I asked,

"We do."

I sent Tylik a bemused look.

"The estate Tylik grew up in is three times the size of this one, and magic swirls everywhere," Finni said. "Here, sadly, we only have access to a speck of magic, mostly charms and spells that are barely worth the effort. Tylik provides the ingredients to cast those spells in his business." She waved to the long room in general and the cabinets lit from within, showcasing endless velvet cases holding jewelry. "Feel welcome to look around. You can touch anything you'd like without receiving a shock."

Shock? Lovely.

Cabinet after cabinet took up most of the walls.

Finni beamed at my amazement. "A bit startling, isn't it, dear?" She put an arm around my waist and gave me a quick hug. "Don't let it intimidate you. This jewelry had been collected over many generations. Most of it is much too gaudy to wear. Once you've finished looking around, I'll show you the rings and you can pick one. Oh, and then we'll find some pretty baubles for you to wear with your beautiful dress."

Overwhelmed already, I slowly walked around the room while Finni and Tylik chatted about who was attending tonight's dinner. From the endless list of names, I suspected my version of a small affair was much different from theirs.

"And your sister has deigned to attend," Finni finished with.

"Isirell will be here?" he asked with excitement. "I haven't seen her in so long."

Finni snorted. "That's not always a bad thing."

"She's fun."

"Mischievous."

"No more than you."

Finni chuckled. Her bright gaze sought mine. "Have you seen anything you like?"

"They're all beautiful."

She walked over to me and directed me to one of the cases. "Rings galore here. Some date back thousands of centuries, though a few are relatively new."

Relatively could mean longer ago than the formation of our country.

"They're all pretty," I said. "What do you like, Tylik?"

His hand dropped onto my shoulder, and he squeezed. He leaned close and pointed. "What about that one?"

It was one of the least gaudy rings on display. My sigh of relief bled out.

Finni opened the top of the case and lifted out the ring, handing it to me.

Made of a simple design, the gold band had been etched with swirls that looked like lettering. Elvish? A solitary clear stone dominated the center, somewhat recessed into the ring rather than rising above it. Smaller blue stones flanked it, two on each side, and they sparkled as if they could generate their own light. The color reminded me of Tylik's eyes. Sapphires?

"Gargoyle made, of course," Finni said with a pert nod. "We wouldn't buy anything less."

Goreg had shared some of his culture with me and Seyla. In the monster world, gargoyles mined and cut most of the stones used to make jewelry, and humans had already caught on to their beauty and value. They drew a very high price, and I couldn't believe I was holding something they'd made.

"I love it," I said, shooting Tylik a smile. I also hoped it wasn't worth a fortune, though I suspected it would take a year's worth of my salary to afford even one item in this room.

"Then it's yours," he said. He took it from me and lifted my left hand.

"What if it doesn't fit?"

"Oh, it will."

"You don't know my size," I teased.

"It's magic."

He slid it onto my finger, and I swore it wiggled, sliding across my skin as if assessing not just the width of my finger but me as well.

Shivers shot through me, and I sucked in a breath when it tightened to the point it wouldn't fall off, but not too snug for comfort.

"It *is* magic," I breathed, admiring it on my finger.

"The magic comes from you, Kate, not the world around you," he said.

CHAPTER 27

TYLIK

After adorning Kate with family jewels, we went downstairs to wait for our guests. My sister, Isirell, popped into the room in the usual way, using magic.

"Isirell," my aunt warned, her worried gaze flicking to the elf guards standing on the opposite side of the foyer. "You must not use that form of magic here."

"Magicking to the border and stepping through the veil, then using a carriage would take forever," Isirell said. "No one will notice a flick of my finger." Her gaze caught mine and, as always, hers was filled with mischief. "Tylik!" She rushed over and hugged me, standing back while bracing my arms to look me over. "You're happy."

I grinned and nudged my head to my fiancée. "This is Kate. Kate? My sister, Isirell." Hopefully the soon-to-be duchess.

"It's wonderful to meet you." Isirell gave Kate a brief

hug, then studied her as intently as she did me. "Thank you for putting a smile on my stoic brother's face."

"I adore your brother," Kate said, warming my heart with her words.

Isi nodded and stepped back. "I think drinks are in order, correct? We can raise a glass to celebrate your upcoming nuptials." She snapped her finger and a tray with three fluted glasses and a bottle of splendeer appeared on a table just inside the parlor.

"Isi," my aunt sighed, her lips thinning. "Please do not."

"No more," Isi said, winking at me. "I promise."

We'd see how long that lasted.

My sister resembled me with the same golden hair and height, though she had our father's black eyes. She'd admired me from the time we were little, following me around everywhere and constantly asking me questions. I hadn't minded too much. I loved her, and I wanted her to be happy. I only had vague memories of our parents; she was too small to remember, and that was a true tragedy.

"You're adorable, little one," our aunt told my sister as we walked into the parlor. "But you try my patience!"

Isi gave Finni a kiss before turning back to Kate, her gaze traveling down my fiancée's front. "You're pretty, soon-to-be sister."

"Isn't she?" Finni asked, opening the bottle of splendeer and pouring glasses for each of us. She handed them around.

"To you, Tylik, and your sweet bride," Isi said, raising her glass.

We entwined our arms, Kate shooting me a grin as we did it, then took sips while still woven together. Unlinking from each other, we stepped backward, settling in seats near the fireplace someone had lit. Flames crackled, and warmth swirled through the room, giving it a cozy feel. Perhaps I did see the value in a fire.

"Are those the Bestilian sapphires you're wearing?" Isi asked Kate.

Kate lightly touched her ring, then the matching necklace and earrings. "They're beautiful. I'm honored to wear them."

"The Bestilian family gifted them to ours three thousand human years ago," Isirell said. "It's only fitting you wear them."

Color rose into Kate's face. "Thank you."

We sipped our drinks and chatted, and I was grateful to see Isi behaving kindly to Kate. My sister could be flighty, but she was endlessly nice. She'd make the perfect duchess once my aunt decided to hand down the title.

Stomps rang out from the front of the estate, and one of the guards swept open the door.

Maxon Zahgorim and his wife, Chastity, bustled inside.

"Whoa," Chastity said, pausing in the open doorway. "Your descriptions made me think this place would be beautiful, but it's stolen my breath." She turned to Max.

"You and your crew did a fantastic job with the construction."

"Yes, he did," Finni said, rising and moving over to greet them. "Welcome. You must give you wife a tour, Maxon."

"If you don't mind, I'll do so later," Max said.

"Of course," my aunt said. "Whenever you'd like. Our humble home is open to you at all times."

Humble? Kate and I shared a grin. This place, a tiny chateau by elf standards, had twenty-five bedrooms, each with ensuite bathrooms.

They joined us in the parlor, and Kate and I rose to greet them.

Max grinned at me and reached out to tap my shoulder. "How are you doing, Tylik? Great to see you again. Kate."

She and Chastity exchanged hugs.

"Good to see you too." This was one of the many reasons why so many loved living here in Monsterville. Here, Maxon ran a construction company. And I was Tylik, the male running the apothecary where other monsters could buy herbal remedies or ingredients for spells. We fit in.

Chastity hugged me after Kate, reinforcing my affection for this community.

"We're having some before-dinner cocktails," my aunt said, gesturing to the splendeer bottle that had magically refilled—as it would do in the fae realm, never here. Another small spell cast by my sister. "I'm sure the rest of the guests will be here soon." Finni nodded to the guards. "Do escort them to us once they've arrived."

"Of course," the guards said in unison.

Before we could sit, the guards swept open the doors again. Raze and Elisa strolled inside and removed their light coats, followed by Gunner and Rylee.

Seyla was with them. She rushed over and gave Kate a hug, then me.

"There you guys are," Elisa said, she and Raze joining us in the parlor.

Gunner dipped his head our way, and Rylee grinned.

"Thank you for the invitation," Raze said, nodding to my aunt and then my sister.

"King Raze?" Isirell asked. "So wonderful to see you again."

"King?" Seyla asked Kate with wide-eyed wonder. Kate shrugged.

"None of that, now." Elisa smirked at Raze. "He's incognito."

"Why?" Isi asked, a light smile on her face.

"I've abdicated the throne," Raze said. "I'm a plain ogre now."

"Never plain, love," Elisa said, and they kissed.

Isi rolled her eyes. "Romance floats in the air, I see."

The front door opened again, and my aunt greeted Grannie Vi and Uncle Bub, who looked amazing in dark blue velvet outfits, Bub wearing a suit and Vi a dress. They paused in the foyer while my aunt gave them each a quick hug.

"This is my fiancée, Elisa," Raze told Isi.

Isi gave Elisa a hug. "Welcome. It's very nice to meet you." Her head tilted as she looked at Raze. "Why abdicate?"

"Because I'm a simple guy," Raze said. His chuckle rang out. "I don't wear suits all the time. I'm done with all that because I love living here, and I don't need anything else. Elisa and I are wedding planners. If you decide to get married, look us up."

Isirell snorted. "I cannot imagine anything like that, but we'll see."

"That's what they all say." Raze lifted his and Elisa's entwined fingers, kissing her knuckles. "Look at me, blissfully happy." He lifted Elisa off her feet and kissed her again.

Kate leaned into my side, and because romance was floating the air, as Isirell had pointed out, I swept her up for a quick kiss that turned into something longer.

"Please," Isi said with a shake of her head. "Save it for after the wedding."

We all laughed.

More guests arrived, joining us in the parlor where we sipped endless splendeer and chatted.

Seyla moved around the room, getting to know everyone. Kate told me her friend had a crush on Vrok, but he didn't seem to feel the same way. I'd thought of telling her to go easy on him, that he was getting over a broken heart, but decided to leave that to them. Seyla didn't seem like the kind who'd give up until she'd tried almost everything, and Vrok might soon change his mind.

"You two didn't find true love through Monster Mingle," Grannie Vi said to me, referring to the match-making service she and her boyfriend, Uncle Bub, had recently opened.

She wasn't my grandmother, and he wasn't my uncle, but everyone in town called them that. They'd officially adopted the entire community, and they were deeply loved by all.

Grannie Vi was Rylee's grandmother, and Bub was Violet's uncle.

"Despite that, we wanted to offer you both a little pre-wedding gift," Grannie Vi finished.

Bub handed me a bright pink bag festooned with ribbons and sealed at the top.

"Please wait to open it until your wedding night," Grannie Vi said with a wink.

"What do you think is inside?" Kate asked, looking at me with complete innocence. She sat on a sofa beside me, driving me to distraction with the simple press of her thigh against mine. We'd been together a day now, but I craved her more than ever.

"Long ago, I was a sex therapist," Vi said, giving Kate a wink as well. "I've got a good eye for what works and what doesn't in the bedroom."

"That you do, Vi. That you do," Bub said with a slow nod. He tapped his temple. "She's brilliant about stuff like that." His gaze fell on my sister. "If you'd like to meet your fated one, come by Monster Mingle, and we'll fix you right up. We've got ogres and orcs, and even a centaur or two that might catch your interest."

"You never know," my sister said with a low laugh.

Kate poked the bag and lowered her voice. "Maybe we should check it out later?"

My pulse roared. "Maybe we should."

CHAPTER 28
KATE

"Tylik," Finni said, waving her half full glass his way. "Would you check with the kitchen to find out how much time we have until dinner?"

"Use magic to do it," Isirell said.

"No," both Tylik and Finni barked.

"I don't mind walking," Tylik said, rising. He shook his finger at his sister, who tried to playfully bite it. "No magic, remember?"

"Boring," she said. Her gaze traveled to the foyer. From the change in the air, someone must've arrived. "There she is. Finally." She rose and rushed across the room, meeting up with Drueline.

"They've been friends since they were little," Tylik told me softly.

From the limpid glance she shot Tylik, followed by a glare at me; I suspected Drueline hoped she and Tylik would end up more than friends.

With a huff, she turned to Isirell, leaning close to whisper something in her ear.

Isi glanced our way and laughed, though the emotion didn't shine in her eyes.

"I'll be right back?" Tylik said, nudging his head in the general direction of the kitchen.

I nodded, and he left.

I sipped my splendeer, though for some reason, it now tasted bitter.

The room quickly filled with various monsters, humans, and more elves than I'd seen in one location in my life. I did my best to remember their names.

Finni kept nodding approval and giving me smiles.

Seyla chatted with a minotaur on the opposite side of the room, and their laughter rang out.

I was beginning to wonder what was taking Tylik so long when Finni rose from her brocade-adorned chair.

"I'd like to show you something in the adjacent parlor, Veskadik," she said to one of the older elves formally dressed in a black tunic and pants. "If you'll attend me."

"Of course, my duchess," Veskadik said, bowing deeply.

Isirell dropped onto the sofa beside me as the two left. "Socializing gets tiring, doesn't it?"

I nodded, not wanting to name how much I wanted to leave with Tylik. We could go home and climb into bed. Snuggle together.

Drueline joined us, standing beside Isi, watching me with a snarky expression while taking sips of her drink.

"Will your family attend the wedding?" Isirell asked me.

"Just my friend, Seyla, who'll be my maid of honor. My mom can't make it."

"I'm sorry. Where does she live?" Isi asked. "I don't know much about the human realm other than that it's as big as the fae world."

"She lives in Chicago. It's a long way from here."

"Has anyone tried to bribe you to skip the wedding?" Drueline asked, her voice coming out sweeter than her words.

"Dru," Isi hissed. She shot me a raised-brow look. "Sorry."

"Excuse me?" I glared at Drueline. Growing up poor, I'd dealt with more than my share of mean girls. It sharpened my wits and taught me how to give whatever they dealt right back.

"I meant," Drueline said, "Has anyone offered you gold coins to break off your engagement?"

"Why would anyone do that?" I asked. Rather bold of her. I peered around, but no one else seemed to be paying attention to our conversation.

"Because it's clear you're marrying Tylik for his wealth." Drueline stared down at her glass as she swirled the liquid. "I could pay you a tidy sum if you'd like. Jewels like the ones you're wearing. Heaps of coins. Spells you could activate whenever you wished."

"I don't want jewelry or spells or money." I only wanted Tylik. A baby would be nice, but I'd want him even if he couldn't give me a child.

"Everyone has their price," she said.

"Dru," Isi said in warning again. "Stop."

"I'm almost done." Drueline snarled at Isi.

"You can't buy me off," I said, rising.

Drueline stared down her nose at me. Damn elves were all so much taller. "Then why marry him?"

I brushed past her, giving her my own human version of a snarl. "Because he's amazing. Get over it, sweetheart."

Seyla caught my eye, and I nodded and tapped my ear; the signal we'd use when we were out and one of us was in trouble.

My friend left the minotaur without a word and scooted over to my side.

"Is Drueline being a pain in the ass? I overheard her whispering about you earlier. Should I stab her now or wait outside the bathroom the next time she uses it and hit her when she comes out?"

"What a nasty piece of work." I explained what Drueline said, feeling bad for Tylik growing up with a woman like that around. It made me feel even closer to him.

It made me want to protect him.

"I'll definitely hit her outside the bathroom, then," Seyla said. She linked her arms on her chest and glared at Drueline.

"She's not worth the jail time."

Seyla wiggled her eyebrows. "You're assuming I'll get caught."

I squeezed her arm. "Thanks for having my back."

"Always."

"I'm going to go find Tylik," I said.

"I'll keep mean girl occupied so she doesn't follow."

While Seyla started toward Drueline, I strode toward the foyer, only to run into Tylik as he entered the room.

He braced my arms and leaned over to kiss me. "Missed you."

And just like that, everything was better.

"If everyone could move into the dining room," Finni announced from the entrance to the other parlor. "Dinner is about to be served."

CHAPTER 29
TYLIK

I'd noted my sister sitting with Kate when I returned to the parlor. I'd also noted Drueline starting at my fiancée with a snarl on her face.

I started toward them, but Kate rose and met me in the entrance to the parlor.

"Are you alright?" I asked, glaring at Drueline.

"I'm fine." She huffed and shook her head.

"We can—"

"Dinner is served," my aunt said.

"Do you want to leave?" I asked.

She shook her head. "Nope. Let's go eat. I'll ignore the witch."

As far as I knew, no witches had been invited tonight, but— Oh, she meant Drueline.

I chuckled. "Yes, let's ignore the witch."

She sent me a true smile.

I held out my arm for her to take. "My lady?"

As per protocol, we followed my aunt as she led everyone to the dining room.

"A few people, huh?" Kate asked me in a shaky voice.

"I would do anything for you, Kate," I said in a deep voice. "If you wish to leave, we will."

"And I'd do the same, which is why we're staying."

We only had to get through this one dinner. Plus the wedding, I supposed, though most of the time, we could be by ourselves.

My aunt took her place at the head of the table, and we sat at her right according to tradition. Other than Isi sitting across from us with Drueline, everyone else sat where they found spots.

Seyla settled into a seat a few down from my right. She peered toward Kate, who nodded, and I was grateful all over again that my fiancée had Seyla for a friend.

I squeezed Kate's hand beneath the table, and while I wanted to take her from the room and anyone who might wish to hurt her, this was a necessary evil.

Elf staff brought out the first course, bowls of a light soup, followed by three small plates of traditional elf appetizers.

Kate kept shooting me smiles, and since I knew how odd some of our food must appear to humans, I discretely answered her grins. I enjoyed having something to share with her; it made a long, boring dinner fun.

After the main course was served, and we'd started eating, Isirell caught Kate's eye.

"I'm sorry your mother can't come to the wedding," Isi said. "We'll be your family, then."

I adored my sister despite her occasional mischief. She had a kind heart, and she never hesitated to show it.

"I'm an only child; it's just me and my mom," Kate said. She lowered her fork with only part of her main course finished.

"Why can't she come?" Drueline asked politely.

Seyla cleared her throat, but other than shooting her a glare, Drueline ignored her.

"She has another event she's attending," Kate said.

"What event could be more important than her daughter's wedding?" Drueline said snidely.

"My mom's special," Kate said firmly. "What she does makes a difference. I don't mind. I'll see her another time."

Drueline snorted.

Why did she think we'd make a good match? I'd more than once noted her cruelty. I hoped she returned to the fae realm soon. She could remain there forever.

"We'll miss your mother," my aunt said. "But we can send her images." She frowned at me. "What are they called?"

"Videos. Photos," I said.

"Yes, that's it."

I could tell she was pleased I knew the answer. Still testing me, it appeared.

"When she watches these images, your mother will feel as if she's there," Finni said.

"That would be wonderful, thanks," Kate said, staring down at her meal.

Isi nodded. She did something to Drueline beneath the table, however, because Drueline released a low yelp and glared at my sister.

Isi ignored her friend and winked at me.

CHAPTER 30
KATE

Seyla left when we did, following us to our place. She bustled inside, carrying a small cake and a gift for me.

"We didn't have time for a bachelorette party, so I'm bringing one to you tonight," she said, handing me the bag.

Tylik watched from where he stood by the fireplace.

"Should I open it now?" I asked.

"Sure." Seyla shot Tylik a grin. "This gift's for you too."

I opened the bag and shifted the tissue paper to the side. My snort of laughter rang out. "You didn't."

"Oh, yeah, I did. Everyone deserves something like this for their wedding night."

I held up the barely there nightie.

Tylik's eyes widened. Was he picturing me wearing it? Because I could imagine myself donning it and strutting around our room for his perusal.

"Thank you." Dropping the gift on the sofa, I rose and hugged my friend. "I'll miss not seeing you all the time."

"Me too," she pretend wailed. Leaning back in my arms, she smiled. "Once I'm settled into my new place, you can come over for barbecues. There's a big ole fence between me and my neighbor, so they won't even know I'm there. As for the neighbor, I never see them. Their truck is gone before I wake up and they don't return until after sundown. Maybe they're a vampire." She shivered. "Which could be fun if I was a night owl, which I'm not."

"We'd love to come over," I said.

We ate big slices of cake in the kitchen, then Seyla left, saying she'd see me in the morning to help me get ready. Tylik promised to rise before me and have Vrok take him to the estate, leaving me here with Seyla.

As I stood in the open doorway, waving as my friend drove away, Tylik came up behind and put his arms around me.

"Would you like me to model my gift?" I asked.

"Tomorrow," he said, sweeping me off my feet. "Right now, I want you completely naked."

WHEN I WOKE the next morning, Tylik had already left, and someone was banging on the front door. I slid from the bed and stuffed my arms through the sleeves of my robe, tying it as I hurried to the door.

"Finally," Seyla said, bustling inside with her arms full of bags and other odd items. "Sleepy head."

"Is that a hula hoop?" I asked, staring at the bright pink ring looped around her arm. "You're helping me get ready, not working out, right?"

"Ha ha. I might." She booted the door shut with her butt and hurried into the living room, laying everything on the furniture. Turning, she frowned at me and pointed her finger toward the hall. "Shower. Now. I'll get everything else ready."

"Yes, Mom," I said with a laugh.

Today was my wedding day, and I was marrying the man—elf—I loved. She could boss me around all she wanted.

It took me longer than normal because I shaved areas I'd never explored with a razor before. Let me tell you, I wasn't looking forward to stubble. But I wanted to be perfect on my special day.

After toweling dry, I dressed in only undies and joined Seyla in the bedroom. She'd removed my gown from the bag and hung it on the back of the closet door.

"It's so beautiful," she said, smiling at me over her shoulder. "You're going to be the prettiest bride in the world."

I rushed over to her and hugged her from behind. "Thank you for helping me get ready."

She patted my arm. "Anytime. Actually scratch that. Let's do this once and not again, okay?"

"That's fine by me. I only want Tylik."

Her grin rose higher. "And he wants you. That's clear."

"I feel so lucky, and I'm afraid." A tremor came through in my voice.

"Why?"

"It feels like things are going too well. You know how my life has been. Nothing stays rosy for long."

"You started over when you came to Monsterville, which means you've set yourself on a new track. Fate wouldn't be so mean to snatch it all away."

Wouldn't it? Fate had taken my father and then my mom from me more times than I liked. I didn't begrudge those she wanted to help. How could I? But sometimes, I wished she had a little more time for me.

"Today's going to be amazing," she said. "Tomorrow's going to be amazing. And each day that follows will be even better. Trust me, will ya?"

"Yes, Mom."

"Now let's get you dressed, do your hair and makeup, and get to the estate."

"You need to get ready too."

She flicked her hand. "Thought I'd go like this." She smirked when I gaped at her cute top and skirt. "Just kidding. Even if I wasn't dressing for your special day— I'm the maid of honor! —I'd dress for your driver."

Vrok would take us to the estate in a limo.

"Let's put on your dress first," Seyla said. She helped me into it, doing up each tiny button on the back. "I'll hand it to the pixies. It fits like a glove." Pivoting me around, she studied my face. "I think light makeup, don't you? We don't want you looking garish."

"You're in charge."

"Finally, you agree!" With a chuckle, she guided me to a chair and made me carefully sit. She worked on my face for a bit, then did my hair. "We're going Brave today, right?"

I thought it was only fitting. I'd found my sword—it resided in my heart—and I would carry it into battle. Today, I'd hold my head high and marry the elf I'd love until my dying day.

And tonight? I'd tell him how I feel.

CHAPTER 31

TYLIK

I dressed in the room my aunt had assigned to me when I'd stayed at the estate in the past, donning a formal tunic and dress pants perfect for one of the highest social events in the elf kingdom.

After, I went downstairs to the parlor to wait.

My aunt joined me, and we sipped small glasses of an elf liquor that had little alcohol but was full of flavor.

"I like Kate," Finni said. "You've done well, nephew."

Soon, Kate would be my wife. My mate. My love for a lifetime.

We hadn't spoken of feelings, but we soon would. I needed to tell her how much she meant to me and how I wanted her by my side forever.

"It's almost time," Raze said from the parlor's doorway. "I believe everything is all set, but I'll zip upstairs to make sure."

Elisa peeked around his bulky body. "You look amazing, Tylik. Ready for wedded bliss?"

"I can't wait." I rose and went to them, rubbing Raze's shoulder and giving Elisa a hug.

They left, and I walked over to my aunt, bending forward to kiss her cheek. "Thank you for everything you've done for me."

She patted my arm. "I'd do it all again. You and your sister have brought joy to my life." She smiled up at me. "Now it's time for you to bring joy to Kate's."

We went upstairs to wait in the library, coming full circle to the place where I'd first met Kate. Had it only been one week since then? It felt like a moment and a lifetime all at once.

"The staff will notify us when she arrives," my aunt said.

"Where's the groom?" someone called out in the hall. Max strode into the room with Chastity who had baby Sydnee in her arms. "The best man is here," he said with a grin, tapping his chest, "Now the wedding can start."

"We're waiting for the bride," my aunt said, rising to go speak with the baby.

Sydnee cooed and kicked her feet while my aunt made cutesy sounds in the child's ear.

We sat and chatted about things I wouldn't remember. All I could think of was what would come next. Excitement poured through me, and my hands shook. I wanted today to go well, not because my aunt would be watching but because this would be a special day for me and Kate.

One of the elf staff stopped in the opening to the library and bowed. "The bride has arrived."

CHAPTER 32

KATE

E lisa was waiting in the foyer. "Kate, you look gorgeous." Tears sprung up in her eyes. "I don't believe I've ever seen a more beautiful bride."

We carefully hugged.

She quickly guided us to the lift Finni used when she wasn't up for climbing stairs, and we squished inside. In no time, we exited on the second level.

"Everyone is inside the ballroom," Elisa said. "But we'll go to the library until we receive our cue."

I paced in front of the fireplace until Seyla hopped in front of me, blocking my passage. "Nervous?"

"How can you tell?" My teeth chattered, and my hands had gone clammy.

"It's going to be a breeze," she said, gripping my upper arms. "Walk down the aisle and make sure you keep your back to the audience."

"Why?"

"If you can't see them, they don't exist."

"Of course they exist. I'll hear them shifting, moving, coughing." Please, no snickering. This had to go perfectly or Finni would haul Tylik back to the fae realm. Since humans were only allowed to travel there under special circumstances, I'd never see him again. "Shit, he's going to divorce me and marry Drueline."

"He is not going to marry Drueline," Seyla said. "Jeez, think about it for one second, would you?"

"What?" Elisa barked. "Why would Tylik marry Drueline?"

"She wants him," I said.

"Does he want her?" Elisa asked softly.

"No, he doesn't." Stating it out loud made my tension ease. I mean, I knew that.

"If he wanted her, he'd be with her," Seyla said. "And he isn't. He only wants you."

"You know why we're getting married," I said.

"Your initial reasons no longer exist."

"You're sure about that?" I asked.

"Well, they do, but things have changed. I've seen how he looks at you. He loves you."

"Do you think so?"

Elisa nodded vigorously. "He's crazy about you."

"Relax if you can," Seyla said. "This is your day, yours and Tylik's. Let's go get you married."

As if on cue, an elf dressed to the hilt in a gleaming tunic and matching pants entered the library and bowed. "It's time. If you'll follow me?"

Elisa handed us our bouquets and wiggled with

excitement. "I'm so happy for you two. Your wedding is going to be amazing."

"See?" Seyla said. "Elisa agrees."

Elisa nodded.

Seyla took my hands and squeezed them. She spread my arms out and scrutinized my appearance, finally nodding. "You're perfect."

I hugged her, squishing our flowers, but I didn't care.

"Ready to be Tylik's wife?" she asked softly.

"I am." Calmness filled me. This was right. *We* were right.

We followed the elf down the hall and stopped outside the closed big double doors. I'd come full circle. A week ago, I'd never imagined I'd be back here to marry a guy I'd fallen in love with.

I was going to go in there and say I do to Tylik.

The music rose inside the ballroom, an elf melody Tylik had requested. He said he remembered his mother playing it on a harp before she died.

"Ready?" I asked Seyla, and she shot me a grin, moving to stand in front of me. Elisa would scoot in through a side door and take her place with Raze near the back so as not to disturb the ceremony.

Elisa gave me a careful hug. "All the best, sweetie. This is your day. Time to shine."

I nodded, and elves opened the doors.

An aisle had been created through the middle of the big ballroom, and guests sat in chairs on either side. From here, it seemed like thousands were in attendance, though from the list, I knew it was only two hundred, a mix of humans, monsters, and numerous elves.

The music paused, and a hush descended. Then the musicians started playing again, and the lilting tune echoed in the high-ceilinged room.

I stepped onto the smooth strip of carpet; my footsteps silent.

Tylik stood waiting at the end of the aisle. He watched me with a gleam of tears in his eyes.

I walked toward him, my steps slow, but with eagerness blooming in my heart. This day was going to be perfect.

I'd nearly reached him when a voice called out from behind.

"I made it, honey!" My mom entered the ballroom. She stopped on the carpet, gazing around in awe before starting toward me. "Sorry I'm late. That elf woman did her best to get me here on time." Shifting one of her canes to the other arm, she waved to Drueline, who smirked.

Damn witch. Why had she done this?

Oh, yes, to humiliate me.

I'd show her.

Mom was dressed in her best, and I'd never seen anyone prettier in my life.

Some of the audience pointed and their eyebrows lifted. To them, her black slacks and bright pink top with a bow must appear comical.

Snickers rang out, growing louder.

I didn't care; I was grateful she was here to share this

day with me. Still, I cringed, because this might be the one thing that would change Finni's mind.

She said no embarrassing incidents. Would she use this against Tylik?

If so, our chance was over already.

CHAPTER 33
TYLIK

"Mom," Kate said, turning. She walked toward a woman who'd stopped on the carpet runner and was peering around in amazement. They had the same red hair and gorgeous eyes. I was so grateful she'd arrived.

Spying Kate, her mother's eyes lit up, and I saw more of Kate in her face. Using two canes, she hobbled toward her daughter with Kate striding toward her mom.

When they met, they hugged.

"I'm so glad you're here. Thank you," Kate said with so much joy it made my chest ache.

"How could I be anywhere but with you on your special day?" Kate's mom said.

The sweetest smile appeared on Kate's face. It made my lungs ache.

"I should introduce her, unlike during our first meeting." Kate's bright laugh rang out. "This is my mom, Willa. Look, Tylik. She made it on time."

"I sure did, honey," Willa said.

"Would you walk me down the aisle, Mom?" Kate asked.

"I'd be happy to walk with you," Willa said.

My aunt sat in the front row, watching me, not my fiancée and her mother. I couldn't read Finni's thoughts from her expression, but I sensed she was making her final judgment.

Fuck it and whatever her decision might be. I controlled my own life; I didn't need my aunt to do it for me. My love, my Kate, was happy. That was all that mattered.

I left the flower-covered archway and strode down the aisle, stopping by Kate as she helped her mom step up beside her.

"She's here," Kate gushed. "She's going to walk me down the aisle. I don't have a dad, but I don't need one. All I need is my mom." With a grin, she flicked her hand my way. "Hey, you're supposed to wait for us at the arch, but if you want to walk with us, that's okay, too." She swallowed, and it appeared to go down hard. Sadness took over her features. "I'm sorry, Tylik. I hope this won't mess things up."

"I don't care," I said. "All that matters is you, Kate. I love you, and I always will. There's no way that could ever be a mistake."

"Tylik," Kate breathed, her eyes shimmering. "I love you too."

My pulse soared, and it was never returning to the Earth again.

"Aw," Willa said. "Is this your fiancé, honey?"

"Yes, Mom. This is Tylik. I love him, and I know you will too."

"Of course I will," Willa said, putting her arm around Kate, giving her a quick hug.

I went around to Willa's other side and held out my arm. "My lady?"

"Look at him," Willa said with a smile that was as achingly beautiful as Kate's. "He's a real gentleman. Oh, gentle-*elf*." She hooked her cane over her forearm and linked her hand through my arm.

Then I walked the love of my life and her precious mother down the aisle.

It was time for us to get married.

CHAPTER 34
KATE

The music rose to a crescendo as we reached the end of the aisle. We paused to help my mom take a seat in the front row next to Finni.

Tylik held out his arm to me. "This isn't a human tradition. I guess we've blown that one out of the water."

Hearing him use a very human statement made my laughter bubble up from deep within me.

"I don't care any longer, do you?" I said.

"As long as you'll be my wife, nothing else matters."

I took his arm, and he escorted me to the archway.

As a justice of the peace, Chastity had offered to marry us.

When we stood before her, she gave us each a big smile.

"Welcome." She lifted her voice. "Welcome all of you. We've come together to join two amazing people and two wonderful worlds, human and elf. And so begins yet another journey, a couple stepping onto the path of love." Her gaze sought Max's, and she gave him a sweet smile.

Tylik held my hand, squeezing it through the service, and when it was time to exchange our vows, he took both my hands, facing me.

"I take you, Kate, to be my wife," he said. "I promise to love and honor you forever." Tears sparkled in his eyes.

"And I take you, Tylik, to be my husband. I promise to love and honor you forever." I didn't try to stop crying. I was messing up Seyla's careful makeup job, but who cared? Tylik had said he loved me, and that was all that mattered.

I had now. Tonight.

If we'd soon be wrenched apart, we'd make memories first that would last both of us a lifetime.

"I now pronounce you elf and wife," Chastity said. "You may kiss to seal your vows."

Tylik lifted me up to his level. "Will you run away with me?"

"What a wonderful idea." I wrapped my arms around his shoulders, and we kissed to the cheers of the crowd.

CHAPTER 35
TYLIK

We walked back down the aisle as elf and wife, and everyone followed us up the grand staircase to the third level where the staff had prepared the second ballroom for our reception. As we sat at the head table, our guests filed in and took seats, Seyla helping Kate's mother before sitting at a table nearby.

"Wife," I said with satisfaction, kissing Kate's hand.

"Husband," she breathed, leaning against me and looking up at me with so much love in her eyes, I wondered how I'd missed it. "Did you mean it when you asked me to run away?"

"I won't go back to the fae realm. My life's here with you."

"Alright, then. We'll do it." She sent me an easy grin. "Where would you like to run to?"

"Wherever you'd like. We have the entire world waiting for us."

"I'm going to miss our hobbit home."

"I'll build you another."

"You're not going anywhere," someone said from behind us. My Aunt Finni placed a hand on each of our shoulders. "You'll remain here in the human realm." She walked around the table to stand in front of us.

Kate watched her with a skeptical expression.

My heart soared because I could see the twinkle in my aunt's eyes. I reminded myself that my sister got her love of mischief from our aunt.

"You never planned to make me take the dukedom," I said, certain of this.

Finni winked. "Nope." She grinned. "Nope is a human word, by the way. I'm learning myself."

"What's happening?" Kate asked, looking between us.

"My poor nephew needed a kick in the—" Finni coughed. "He needed to be prodded. I hoped he'd find someone at Vi's matchmaking service, but he was not successful there. So I decided to do some matchmaking myself." She nodded to Kate. "I'd seen you around town, and after my nephew gawked at you in the ballroom, I called him to the library. You see, I'd already seen you enter, and I knew you were hiding behind the draperies."

"This was all an elaborate matchmaking game from the start?" Kate asked.

"It went splendidly, didn't it?" Grannie Vi said, using her cane to join us. Uncle Bub was right behind her. "We were in on it too."

She and my aunt made a strange gesture to each other, lifting their palms and slapping them together.

"One more down, and many more to go," Bub said. "I was thinkin' of poor Vrok. I believe he also needs an intervention."

"You are so right, Bub. So right," Vi said. She shot me a grin. "You're not upset with how this came out, are you?"

"Not one bit." I turned to my bride. "We married under odd circumstances, but I'm asking you now; will you be my forever love, Kate?"

"Tylik?" she said, tugging me down for a quick kiss. "I thought you'd never ask."

CHAPTER 36
EPILOGUE: KATE

Later that day.

"Can I take the blindfold off now?" I asked Tylik.

"Not yet," he said. "Once we land." He leaned close. "Unless you'd like to continue wearing it. Have you ever imagined what it would be like to be tied to a bed, blindfolded, while I love your body?"

A shiver tracked through me. "I haven't, but now I am." My core throbbed already, and I couldn't wait until we were alone and could get naked.

After the reception, which turned into a huge party of monsters and elves and humans all eating and dancing together, we'd said goodbye and left in a flisteer carriage for our honeymoon.

Drueline, thankfully, fled before we reached the reception. I hoped we never saw her again.

Mom had taken time off from work and her volunteer duties, and she was going to stay with Finni at the estate for a while. We'd visit together when we returned from our honeymoon.

And she was talking about moving to Monsterville, stating she'd seen a lovely animal shelter in town, plus other charities where her work was needed.

She'd already promised to come for the holidays, and she and Finni had reserved her a suite on the third floor of the estate.

The carriage dropped to the ground. I felt it in my belly and in the thump when the wheels settled.

"Where are we?" Curiosity was eating me alive.

"Almost there," Tylik whispered, his voice full of mischief. He got that from his aunt.

I shifted around until I could climb onto his lap, straddling him and cupping his face. "Tell me."

He kissed my palms. "You won't convince me to share that easily."

A bit of wiggling might convince him.

Soon, he was groaning. "You're trying to distract me, wife," he said, his voice sexy and growly.

"I'm glad it's working."

"You'll always be able to seduce me."

"And you me."

The carriage came to a halt.

"We're here," Tylik said, his voice filled with excitement.

"Can I take off the blindfold now?"

He untied it and slid it off my face. "We'll hold onto that for later."

Definitely. He might enjoy being blindfolded himself.

I slid off his lap, and he opened the carriage door. With the windows covered with fabric, I couldn't see where we were, but it smelled unlike anything I'd experienced before.

Tylik stepped outside. He took my hand, urging me to join him. "My lady?"

"The fae realm?" I stared around in awe. "It's just like the scene in your painting."

"Including the cabin." He gestured to the building nestled in the woods. "I got permission for you to travel here. It's time to start our honeymoon, love."

He led me across the grass, and while I had to pause here and there to say hi to pixies and converse with a tree, we finally made it to our honeymoon suite—a cute, ten-room "cabin" within the fae realm.

Tylik swept me off my feet and carried me inside the building.

———

I hope you've enjoyed Tylik & Kate's story
as much as I did writing it.

Next is Seyla & Vrok's romance!
You can find My Orc-y Break Heart

on Amazon.

Check out the rest of the Monsterville, USA world:
Candy For My Orc Boss, Max & Chastity
Orc Me Baby One More Time, Gunner & Rylee
Gargoyles Just Want to Have Fun, Goreg & Violet
Don't Go Knotting My Heart, Storm & Luna
Whose Bed Have Your Claws Been Under, Darrow &
Paige
Uptown Ogre, Raze & Elisa
My Orc-y Breaky Heart, Vrok & Seyla
Hold Me Closer, Fiery Phoenix, Nyxor & Brooke
& Who Let the Demon Out?
(Venom & Ali's story)

Would you like a FREE book?
Sign up for my newsletter, and
I'll send you Escorting the Alien,
a complete, HEA romance.

About the Author

Ava Ross is a two-time *USA Today* Bestselling author who has written numerous titles, all of them featuring sweet and steamy romance. She fell for men with unusual features when she first watched Star Wars, where alien creatures have gone mainstream. She lives in New England with her husband (who is sadly not an alien, though he is still cute in his own way), her kids, and a few assorted pets.

SERIES BY AVA

Mail-Order Brides of Crakair

Brides of Driegon

Fated Mates of the Ferlaern Warriors

Fated Mates of the Xilan Warriors

Holiday with a Cu'zod Warrior

Galaxy Games

Alien Warrior Abandoned

Beastly Alien Boss

Bride of the Fae

A Sci-Fi Holiday Tail

Monsterville, USA

Monster on Board
(co-written with Alana Khan)

A Monster Worth Fighting For
(Monster Between the Sheets)

Love at First Orc

Third Galaxy on the Left

Monster Mate Hunt

You can find her books on Amazon.

MY ORC-Y BREAKY HEART

Can I convince my hot orc neighbor we're meant to be together?

My hunky orc neighbor, Vrok, who I'd love to get to know better, keeps ignoring me.

When he overhears me reading the draft of my steamy romance novel aloud, he tells me he has ideas to make the male point of view better.

One thing leads to another, and soon we're not only reciting the dialogue in my book, we're acting out the most of the scenes.

Between bringing him cookies and mowing his back lawn to thank him, I'm determined to show him I'm special. I'm rewarded when somewhere between Chapter fifteen and a troll roller coaster ride, we start falling for each other. Then matching mate bond symbols appear on our wrists.

Now we can't tell what's real and what's not. If we break the bond, will we still be in love?

My Orc-y Breaky Heart, Book 8 in the Monsterville, USA Series, is a spicy monster romcom. Each book is stand-alone and best if read in order (see below). Expect romantic hijinks with monsters, heat, and a happily ever after.

Turn the page for Chapter 1 . . .

CHAPTER 1
VROK

I stepped out into my backyard to let my dragonette pet, Merith, do his thing in the grass—which was better than doing it mid-flight where it more often than not plopped on my head.

After placing him on the lawn that needed mowing, I sat on my back steps. My small, dragon-like creature hopped around, eating bugs. Sunlight gleamed off his golden scales, and it didn't take more than him shooting me a dragon-y grin for my heart to melt, just like it had when I picked him out of the litter.

"Yes, you're my true love, the only one I'll ever crave," a woman's voice said nearby with so much passion, it made my pulse come to a jarring halt.

Swallowing hard, I glanced toward the tall wooden fence separating my back yard from the one next door. The house had sold a month or so ago, and my new neighbors had settled in. Since I was busy building my fledgling security business, I hadn't gone over to meet the new owner yet.

"I long for the days when we'll be together always," she said with in a heady voice. "So much. I promise I won't allow him to control me much longer. Soon I'll be free, and we'll be together."

"He will not control you at all," a deeper voice growled. "I'll protect you, my precious one."

Kissing sounds punctuated the air.

I shrunk on my back deck. Since I was one of the biggest orcs in our community, I couldn't completely hide, but jeez. PDA much? Good thing a tall fence separated my back yard and theirs.

Merith cocked his head, staring toward our neighbor's place.

"I'll kill him," the male voice said with a snarl.

My eyes widened. Not long ago, I'd worked for the local police force. I'd left to start a security business, though I didn't investigate murders. Was I about to find myself overhearing a plan to commit a horrendous crime?

"Please, don't risk yourself," she said. "He's not worth it. You could be caught."

"I'm good at hiding things like that," the guy said.

Whoa.

"No." Her voice lifted. "You can't. If he finds me, I'll gather my stuff together and escape the city. If I travel far enough, he'll never find me."

Monsterville wasn't quite what I'd call a city; more

like a small town. But who was I to say? It was all about perspective.

"Love me, precious one," she cried. "Love me. Make me forget about him. I don't want him coming between us any longer."

At least they'd moved on from plotting murder.

There was no escaping the conversation until Merith finished on the lawn. I waved my claws toward him, hoping he'd get the message and do his thing so I could slink back inside. There was no way I wanted to sit out here while they did something sexual.

Moans and kissing sounds swept over the fence.

Take it inside, folks?

"Our love will stand the test of time," the guy said, and my heart pinched.

You'd think I'd be over my longing for love and romance by now. My ex had ripped my heart out by the roots when she left me. Why would I want to sow a new seed?

"You're my passion," he said. "My only reason for existence."

Clichéd, but who was I to comment? The only serious relationship I'd had crashed and burned to ashes a few months ago. If I had my say, I'd never open my heart to anyone other than friends, family, and pets again.

Moans and groans echoed from my neighbor's yard, telling me the guy's words were a success. Maybe if I'd laid it on thick like that, Margie wouldn't have ditched me while we were planning our wedding.

"Complete me, love," the woman said. "Show me how much I mean to you."

The woman's voice should not spark need inside me. She wasn't speaking to me.

"I have no intention of doing anything else," the guy said. "First, I'll strip your clothing from your body and lick you until you scream."

Hell, no, I didn't want to listen to this.

My cock should not twitch. Ugh. Neighbor porn in action.

"Hurry up, Merith," I said softly, but my infernal pet kept clawing at the ground, seeking bugs.

Hopefully, I could retreat inside before anything too hot happened, because there was no way I'd sit around listening to something like that.

Bangs rang out as if someone was dragging a chair across a deck. Shit, they were going to do it out in the open and during broad daylight? Their yard was fenced, but the homes in this area were pretty much built on top of each other.

Rising, I crept toward Merith.

Spying me approaching, he took flight. After what I swore was a conniving look thrown my way, he swooped up and over the fence, disappearing into my neighbor's back yard.

A yelp rang out.

Now I'd done it. Just call Merith a cockblocking neighbor.

Wincing, I strode to the gate connecting the two back yards, making a lot of noise to announce I was coming.

The former owners of both places used to be best friends and had the gate installed. I'd intended to put a lock on my side but hadn't found the time. I'd add it to the list of the things I still needed to do at my place.

Once my business was running smoothly, I could slow down and make more time for stuff like that.

I creaked the gate open and paused to give my neighbors time to yank on clothing or cover up.

"I'll just grab Merith and go back inside," I said loudly for the same reason. "Sorry to disturb you folks. I . . . didn't hear a thing." Yeah, sure.

Merith had landed on my neighbor's grass but instead of seeking a snack, he was hopping toward someone sitting—*alone*—on the back deck. With the sun in my eyes, I couldn't see who it was.

"Come on, Merith," I said. "Let's leave these two alone."

"Two?" a woman said.

I knew that voice. It had haunted my dreams since I met her.

Seyla Anderson, the best friend of my friend, Tylik's new wife.

From the moment I saw her, I'd craved her. She'd made it clear she was interested, and I'd done my best to shut her down. My wounded heart couldn't handle another breakup.

Jealousy I had no right feeling surged inside me, followed by a tinge of disgust. Seyla had made it clear she was interested in me while all the time she was professing undying love to someone else?

My ex was bad, but not like this. Talk about fickle.

"Two as in you and your . . . *partner*," I said. Husband? If so, it was even worse. Disgust came through in my growl. "You've got some nerve, Seyla."

"What do you mean, Vrok?"

"You know what I mean." I grabbed Merith and lifted him, placing him on my shoulder where he spent most of his waking hours.

Instead of clinging to my shirt as usual, he flapped his wings, taking flight. He soared over to land on Seyla's lifted hand.

She carefully shifted a laptop onto a table beside her lounge chair. "Nice to see you again, Merith," she cooed to my pet.

My dragonette purred and stretched out his neck to rub his face against hers. Her laughter rang out, the sound tickling down my spine.

I shook my head and stomped my big feet. "You . . . you . . . . You made a play for me while you're obviously in a relationship," I said. It wasn't my place to let the guy know she was a cheater, but buyer beware and all that. He must've slunk inside the house.

Seyla released another low, husky laugh that made my skin twitch. "You think I'm with someone?"

"I heard him. He wants to lick you."

So did I.

I tried to ignore how gorgeous this female was from her long brown hair shot through with natural golden highlights, to her curvy shape and the tiny dimple in her right cheek. Her brown eyes with really long lashes completed the perfect package.

Still chuckling, she rose and walked toward me with Merith perched on her hand. "I'm alone here."

"You were about to do something with another guy."

Her snort rang out. "You almost sound jealous."

I huffed. "Why should I be?"

She shrugged. "I'd like to think it's because you like me, but you ignored me when I . . . as you say . . . made a play for you." Her glance took in her laptop. "There's no one here but me. I was reading my latest book out loud."

"Your book?"

"I'm a romance author. I'll be publishing this one in a few months. I'm doing a solid edit right now. It helps to read it out loud. I find so many mistakes that way."

"Wait, you weren't planning to murder someone?"

She snorted. "Not so far."

"And you weren't about to have wild sex on your back deck with a guy?"

"No one I'm interested in has offered me wild sex yet." Her heated gaze traveled down my frame, and my cock kicked into action. "Are you offering?"

"Of course not," I bellowed.

Her lips twisted. "You could let me down easy."

Flustered, I could barely think, let alone talk. Back to her book. That, I might be able to discuss in a reasonable tone of voice.

I was not tempted to rip off my clothing and take her up on her possible offer. Or maybe I was.

"You don't have the guy's words right," I blurted out.

Her hand snapped to her hips, and fury lit up her pretty eyes. "I imagine you think you can do it better."

Oh, I could do *it* better, but she'd never find out.

Before I could hold the word back, they popped from my mouth. "Why don't I help you with the guy's dialogue?"

Pick up your copy of My Orc-y Break Heart NOW!